CIVIL SERVICES

Challenges and Resolutions

CIVIL SERVICES

Challenges and Resolutions

(A COMPARATIVE STUDY OF BUREAUCRACIES OF INDIA, USA AND CHINA, THEIR GROWTH EVOLUTION AND WORKING)

YOGENDRA NARAIN, IAS (Retd.)

PRABHAT
PAPERBACKS

Published by
PRABHAT PAPERBACKS
An imprint of Prabhat Prakashan Pvt. Ltd.
4/19 Asaf Ali Road,
New Delhi-110002 (INDIA)
e-mail: prabhatbooks@gmail.com

ISBN 978-93-90900-21-3
CIVIL SERVICES: CHALLENGES AND RESOLUTIONS
by Yogendra Narain, IAS (Retd.)

Edition
First, 2021

Price
₹ 295.00 (Rupees Two Hundred Ninety Five only)

Printed at
R-Tech Offset Printers, Delhi

"This book is dedicated to my wife Neena,
My brother Surendra Narain Mathur,
My sisters Swarup Lata Mathur
and Late KusumMathur".

Preface

Future societies will be significantly different from our current societies. The primary reasons for this include slow economic growth, an ageing population, increased frequency and intensity of natural disasters and instability in energy supply and demand. Other factors include the development of smart devices, reduced consumption patterns, sluggish investment, income disparity and the decline in employment. Consequently, governments around the world will be confronted with new demands and expectations, and the repercussions of a fast-growing array of new technologies and tools. Hence, for governments to be efficient and effective in today's complex, interlinked and fast-changing environment, they will need to redesign their structures and processes to capitalise on a new set of actors and tools. More importantly, due to the Internet and the social networking revolution, future governance might not be in the hands of the government alone. Technology has empowered ordinary citizens by offering them a means to make their voices heard and to challenge government leaders regarding their ability and willingness to address public concerns and requests. Therefore, the future of governance lies in networks that include government, business, non-governmental organisations and civil society on multiple scales and levels, from global institutions to neighbourhoods and tribal councils. Locating the most effective nexus of particular activities and understanding how governance works in this new complex ecosystem are central to future governance. They need to remain relevant by being responsive to these rapidly changing conditions and citizens' expectations. They also need to build their capacities to operate effectively in complex, interdependent networks of organisations and systems across public, private and non-profit sectors to co-produce "public value".

In this context, the civil service systems, in most countries, require considerable modernisation. Current civil service systems are traditionally structured, rigid, inward-looking and based on outdated competencies. In addition to increasing their networking and collaboration capabilities, governments need to be more transparent, flexible and participatory. Thus, measures to align civil service systems with these new characteristics are required. To predict the role of civil servants and the direction of personnel policy in the future, it is necessary to grasp the major trends, events and issues, and the scientific and technological developments and ideas that will most likely affect societies of the future. Future societies are expected to be matrix societies in which individuals can choose and combine their own preferences.

Global competition is expected to intensify, while technical and institutional trade barriers are gradually eliminated. Production and trade of goods and services and the movement of production to lower income countries are also expected to escalate. In this respect, due to the influence of globalisation, the nation-state as the basic unit of the world order during the period of industrialisation will lose its authority. Meanwhile, those who have gained positive experiences from the culture of other countries will be critical of the problems their own governments will be confronted with, raising the requirements for active improvement of government services. In addition, cloud computing accelerates the capabilities of digital technologies. Remote computing services allow mass collaboration around huge data sets and in terms of scale to computationally make intensive problem-solving affordable.

Data are viewed as tradable assets and most consumers collect, track, barter or sell their personal data for savings, convenience and customisation, thereby making information a form of currency in the truest sense. These factors have implications for how future public officials will work in harmony with machines.

These trends and drivers could have the implications for the public service in the near future. In future societies, governments will co- produce public value by building collaborative capabilities that can work effectively through complex, interdependent networks and systems encompassing public, private and non-profit organisations. This change in the value production system will require both a new form of government and organisational change. In most cases, government services will be commercialised and will compete with the private sector. In future societies, governmental administration services may be unable to compete, if they do not, or cannot, provide good quality services at low prices.

Disruptive technological innovations including nanotechnology, artificial intelligence (AI), robot technology fused with living matter, information technology (IT) and biotechnology will change the paradigms in various scientific fields. As such, governments should abolish policies that reduce or hinder international competition and use selection and concentration to ensure successful continuation into the future. In this context, governments will need to adopt improved and specialised education and training policies to attract the type of public officials necessary for future societies. These public officials will need to drive network governance while adapting to new environmental changes and technological developments. Management officials, in particular, should develop their global network capabilities with counterparts from civil society, private companies and other countries. The civil service systems of most countries require considerable modernisation. Current civil service systems are traditionally structured, rigid, and inward-looking and based on outdated competencies.

In addition to being more transparent, flexible and participatory, governments need to increase their networking and collaboration capabilities and capacity. Therefore, measures that will align civil service systems with these new characteristics are required. Pressure to decrease the size of the civil service in some countries should not be confused with the need for modernisation; however, as although they may seem related, these issues are separate. In addition, the operations of most public service systems are based on civil service laws created decades ago. In most cases, the legislation does not provide the civil service with the authority or flexibility to share information or engage with the business and non-profit sectors for the co-production of public goods. Consequently, this unfolding reality will require public service systems to become innovative in adapting to the needs, expectations and demands of future generations. Hence, any modernisation requires special programmes that teach public management, while guiding employees to work proactively and collaboratively.

Future governments should draw their personnel from all sectors of society, particularly at the managerial level, and facilitate the movement of HR to and from the civil service and other sectors of the economy and society. In this sense, traditional bureaucracy should be dismantled creatively and a new HR system should be established. Creative dismantling is a change in the existing personnel paradigm through the introduction of a personnel system that fits the future system.

It is necessary to establish an organisational culture and infrastructure that pursues continuous change and innovation. It is difficult to reform the bureaucracy without changing its organisation; also it is necessary to establish a public talent ideal in accordance with future environmental changes and the composition of government organisations. The term "public talent ideal" does not refer to a model or the most optimised talent; rather, it refers to the talents and competencies needed for the form of government necessary to successfully operate in the environment of the future.

Therefore, personnel systems should adapt accordingly, so that they are compatible with creative and innovative public officials. Bureaucracy will undergo creative dismantlement. "Creative dismantling" refers to a state in which the old paradigm has been completely removed so that a new paradigm can be developed. This will not result in the collapse or disintegration of the bureaucracy, because if the bureaucracy disappears, the meaning of public office will too. Rather, the bureaucracy will continue to exist, as an "artificial intelligence bureaucracy" that liberates human beings from traditional bureaucracy. This AI bureaucracy will emerge due to its ability to deliver values of "efficiency" and "legitimacy" at the same time.

Even recruitment systems, including examinations and interviews, should be modernised to facilitate the recruitment of employees with new competencies and skills. In addition to knowledge, selection methods should assess the attitudes and behaviour of candidates. Job descriptions for posts should not apply or reflect a rigid framework within which management and staff are unable to operate with flexibility and initiative. Although advancement in the public sector is often linked to seniority, criteria rewarding efficiency, effectiveness and initiative should be given greater significance in the promotion of staff. Moreover, remuneration systems should be able to reward civil servants who are particularly effective, innovative and engaged.

In the future, AI will constitute the most logical and secure alternative in running day-to-day public service operations. However, AI is incapable of distinguishing mistrustful thinking or mischievous choices, as it cannot venture beyond rationality by default.

A "pathfinder type talent" is a person who is capable of being flexible and responsive to uncertain and rapidly changing environments. In this context, this type of person is not limited by a formal and retentive way of thinking and behaviour; instead, he or she can present an alternative vision and lead adventure and change.

An individual possessing this type of talent will most likely have a strong will to both challenge and pioneer changes in the increasing uncertainty of the future environment and possess the ability to make quick and accurate situational judgements. Furthermore, this type of talented individuals will gain people's trust by implementing policies, in a timely fashion, displaying excellent intuition and responsiveness, even in unexpected environmental changes. Moreover, this type of individual will have the curiosity to find out what is natural and the ability to discover the hidden problem. Centralized supervision of such large numbers does not promise to be easy. Globally, centralization has been observed to militate against diversity of thought. And that's vital to the governance of a country like India.

India, USA and China represent three different systems of governance. India is a democracy with a parliamentary system of governance, While USA is a democracy with a presidential system of governance and China on the other hand is a unitary state, with an authoritarian political structure, dominated by a single party, known as the Chinese Communist Party. India has multiple political parties, while USA has a two-party system. In India and USA, the people choose their political leaders by voting, whereas in China, there are no general elections, in which the citizens participate to elect their governments.

India's civil service is based on the Weberian model, independent of political leanings. Western Europe and the

United States civil services have gone through stages or phases from civil servants being perceived as personal servants of the crown to civil servants as state servants, to civil servants as public servants. The historical development of the civil service in China however has departed substantially from this model. Because of the importance of Marxist definitions of the state in China, functionaries serve the proletarian state, which exercises dictatorship over class enemies. It does not have an independent or an apolitical civil service.

India, as a country, in its present phase of history, is only 73 years old Its civil service was originally based on the British Indian civil service. Over the years, however it has been reoriented to developmental administration. While in India all the recruitments to government services are through independent examination with merit as the criteria, in USA there are still direct political appointments at the upper levels, while the rest are recruited on merit through examinations. USA as an independent nation is more than 240 years old and its civil services has taken shape as per the needs of the times; In China however, most of the appointments are based on loyalty to the Chinese communist party with a thin veneer of merit.

This book attempts to find out how the bureaucracies function in the different and widely varying political environment of these three countries and which functions more effectively.

Acknowledgements

I would like to acknowledge the pivotal role played by my long-term friend and senior journalist Sri Gopal Misra who inspired me to write this book during the lock down period because of Covid-19. He contributed substantially in correcting and improving the drafts and giving me new ideas on the subject matter of the book. He also ensured that I keep to the deadlines fixed by him.

I would also like to thank my children Deepak, Ashish and Aparna for collecting the reading materials which provided the base for this book.

I would also to thank the Director and Librarians of Indian Institute of Public Administration, New Delhi for identifying the relevant literature relating to the civil services of the three countries.

I would also to thank Manan Dwivedi, Asst. Professor in IIPA, who helped in collecting literature on civil services of USA.

I also want to thank the department of Political Science, Allahabad University headed by the late Sri AB Lal for embedding in me, in the early sixties, a love for constitutional studies and introducing me to the philosophies of political thinkers.

Contents

CHAPTER 1

Historical Evolution of Bureaucracy in India

The evolution of civil services in the two biggest democracies of the world, India and USA, had their beginnings in the search for new territories and new trade channels, by British adventurers.

In India, initially the European powers came in the quest for spices and trade. They had encountered in India a well-developed civilization and powerful kingdoms. The Portuguese had reached the Malabar Coast (Kerala) much before the establishment of the factories and trade offices of the British. It took the London based corporate, East India Company (EIC), a prolonged period of twelve years to seek permission from the Mughal court to trade and set up factories. But once permission was given to set up their headquarters at Surat, the East India Company (EIC) also established trade offices in Madras (now Chennai) and Calcutta (now Kolkata).

The difference was that in the case of USA, the explorers had reached the New World to colonise the vast American continent. They were settlers who had crossed the Atlantic to search for a new life after consciously leaving Britain, their homeland. But the important point to remember is that both in the case of India and USA, the settlers were from Britain and their ideas of governance and administration came from there.

The East India Company was established in Britain as a mercantile company for trade in 1600 AD. In fact, the company received a Royal Charter from Queen Elizabeth on 31st December, 1600. It was incorporated by a group of rich London based merchants. In 1612, it was made a joint stock company. It meant that the investments in shares need not be returned. The company appointed factors to look after their factories and warehouses. These factors may be called the first civil servants of the company. Since the appointments in India were quite lucrative, the aspiring factors had to bribe the directors of the company in London, to get these jobs. Much later on, the company getting to know of this corruption, discontinued the system of nominations, and decided to take fresh civil servants on the basis of passing out successfully from the famous Hailebury College in UK.

With the decline of the Mughal Empire in India and more conquests in other parts of the country, the East India Company decided to make Calcutta, the capital of the growing British Empire in India. Calcutta became a flourishing centre of trade, after the defeat of Siraj-ud-

Daula, the Nawab of Bengal, in the famous battle of Plassey in June 1757. With the further decline of the Mughal throne in Delhi, the Governors and Rulers of Hyderabad, Oudh and Bengal became independent rulers. During the next 100 years, the East India Company became the sole sovereign authority of India after seizing power from the native rulers. In the initial years, the Company had obtained sanction from the Mughal rulers as well as the British crown to raise an army to protect its factories and establishments. As the Company expended its territories, a vast administrative set up was also required. The British system of governance was blended with the traditional system then prevailing in the country and governance was established. The French system of commissioners used by Napolean Bonaparte, to govern far flung areas was also adopted. A Governor General was appointed as the head of the local British administration in India.

During the first 150 years of the East India Company, the latter functioned as the subordinate of the Mughal authority. It was called the Company Sarkar Bahadur, ba-Hukam Badshah (By order of the Emperor). During these years, the Company could rule India under the sovereign authority of the Mughal Government. The civil servants of the company had to keep this factor in mind.

During this period, the Industrial Revolution had taken place in UK and Europe. This empowered the mercantile classes in England to become capitalist. They needed a captive market. It unleashed repression and destruction of the cottage industries across India. Vast agricultural lands began to be used for exports, whether it was opium or tea. The civil servants of the company evolved cost effective governance systems. It was basically repressive and a profit-oriented system. In the company government, Indians were recruited, but mostly to serve as subordinates. Later on, they were given higher positions in what were called covenanted services.

With the company's unprecedented territorial expansion in India, the State systems had to be evolved. It needed a vast system to be manned by competent people, including punishments to be meted out, wherever necessary. The Regulating Act of 1773 was the first landmark in the history of Public Administration in the country. It led to the foundation, though with a humble beginning, of the present administrative set up in India. The administration of the country was to be supervised with the setting up of the Supreme Authority, i.e. the Governor General, the Central Government and the provincial Governments. The first Governor General was Warren Hastings, who had a council of three members, all covenanted servants. Under this act, a Code of Conduct was also prescribed for the civil servants.

The Regulating Act of 1773, heralded the formation of a civil service on a pattern consistent with the principles of honest public administration. All top Indian officials were dismissed and any job with more than 500 pounds a year as a salary was reserved for the Company's civil servants, who were European. The higher officers were to be Europeans and the subordinates were Indians, as they were perceived to be more suited for the detailed field work of the district. It was not till the later part of the nineteenth century that Indians were permitted to enter the civil service at the higher levels. Economy and simplicity were the watchwords of the various branches of the administrative system. An efficient system of vigilance was also established.

Warren Hastings introduced the office of the District Collector in 1772. This was one of the most powerful posts in the entire British Empire. It was to be manned by the civil servants of the Company. This officer had multiple responsibilities as Collector; he was the head of the revenue organization, charged with registration, alteration and partition of holdings; the management of indebted estates; the settlement of disputes; loans to agriculturists, and famine relief.

As District Magistrate, he exercised general supervision over the inferior courts, and in particular directed the police work. On behalf of the Company he was responsible for keeping peace in his area and later became the general controlling authority over all departments in his district. The British made the district as the basic unit of administration.

The East India Company also gradually built up a private army of 2,60,000 soldiers and officers, almost twice the size of the then British Army by 1803. The effective rule of the Company had begun in 1757 with the Annexation of Bengal and ended following the 1857 uprising against its repressive regime. The British called this uprising as the Mutiny, whereas the Indians call it the First War of Independence.

The British Government then moved in speedily in 1857 after the mutiny and nationalized the assets of the Company. The spoils system of recruiting senior civil officials for India was replaced by a merit-based examination in London. Since then all selections of civil servants were based on merit. This pattern of recruitment of civil servants to manage the higher echelons of administration continued till 1947 and after India attained Independence, is continuing till now.

The concept of the modern Civil Services, recruited on merit, took place after the British Government took over all the assets of the East India Company in 1857. It must be mentioned however that even prior to the British coming in India in 1600, some forms of civil services always existed at the time of the Mauryan Empire, the Gupta Empire, Republics of the Licchavis and of course the Mughals. In fact, the first well known land revenue system was conceptualized and implemented at the time of Emperor Akbar by Todar Mal. These civil servants were responsible for the collection of the land revenue, other revenues in the nature of custom and excise duties etc. Without money, neither the State, nor the armed forces, nor the other functionaries of Government could survive. Of course, in those times all the civil services posts were manned by favourites of the rulers and their chief trusted advisors.

The uprising that took place in India in 1857, had jolted the British Government in London. It realized that a vast country like India cannot be administered through a private corporate. The finances of the East India Company also suffered. The British forces crushed the rebellion. They also dethroned the last of the legitimate rulers of India, Emperor Bahadur Shah Zafar, and exiled him to Myanmar (Burma). In an effort to give a sense of belonging to the Indians and loyalty to the British crown, Queen Victoria issued a proclamation declaring Indians as her Majesty's subjects. The Governor General was redesignated as the Viceroy of India, representing the British monarch. He was declared as the Supreme Administrator of British India and all the civil servants, as well as the military, came under him. Thus, the territories of the East India Company were forfeited and co-opted in the British Empire. The administration of India was formally and legally transferred from the private company to the Crown.

A Board of Revenue manned by civil servants was set up and all District Magistrates had to report to the Board. The District Magistrates were responsible for collecting information about what was happening in their district. An Accounts Department, including the Pay Masters office were set up.

There was a clear demarcation of the duties and responsibilities within the Company administration. A company employee could either adopt the commercial side or the administrative, for working, but not both. The civil servants of the company, became the eyes and ears of the Governor General and loyal and dedicated agents and executors of the policies.

The Indian Administration

The powers related to revenue, civil Justice and magistracy were fully and unambiguously vested in the collector. He had the authority to arrest and to decide cases both civil and criminal cases.

The collector was expected to tour his district intensively. He had to coordinate the work of the various departments of the government in the district. However, with the setting up of representative institutions, especially civic bodies, the executive authority was shared. Initially, these local bodies were having only British members, but with the participation of Indians, its representative character had increased. The first local body out of the British Isles was the Madras Municipal Corporation, now Greater Chennai Corporation. It was constituted in 1688. According to the British documents, its aim, initially, was to check the unbridled powers of the then Governor of Madras, Elihu Yale. However, it led to the setting up more and more civic bodies across the country. With the constitution of the local district boards and municipalities for the first time, civil servants too had to deal with elected representatives.

The Indian bureaucracy was assigned two key responsibilities, the task of policy making and its implementation. These twin roles continued till the introduction of diarchy under the Government of India Act 1919. The civil servants now had to face political leaders within the administrative system. In a bid to avoid any confrontation within the system between the elected authority and the officials, legal protection was given to the members of civil services.

The Government of India Act 1919 stated in section 96B

"Subject to the provisions of this Act, and of rules made there under, every person in the Civil Service of the Crown in India holds office during his Majesty's pleasure, and may be employed in any manner required by a proper authority within the scope of his duty". The same provision continued in the Government of India Act 1935. However, the provincial governments were allowed to recruit their officers and these officers were too were extended the similar protection. In the Government of India Independence Act 1947, all officers recruited by the Secretary of State were given protection, as far as their salaries were concerned. These provisions were also incorporated in the Constitution of India.

With the Declaration of the Second World War, the Congress Ministries, elected under the provisions of the Government of India Act 1935, resigned in all the provinces. The Governors of the various States, who were originally civil servants, took over the reins of administration. The civil servants in the state secretariats and in the field regained their independent role and played a key-role in helping the war preparations till 1945. However, with the formation of the interim government, the civil servants once again started functioning under the ministers. A year later, a much more challenging task awaited them.

The twin states, India and Pakistan, came into being by the Indian Independence Act 1947 enacted in the House of Commons. Many believe that it was a peaceful transfer of power from the colonial authorities to the Indians, but it was, perhaps more traumatic than the suffering of the American settlers seeking independence from Britain. The British conceded the United States Declaration of Independence, pronounced at the Second Continental Congress held at the Pennsylvania State House (now known as Independence Hall) on July 4, 1776. Seven years later, the British formally recognized the independence of America, when the Treaty of Paris was signed on September 3, 1783. In 1947, the dawn of freedom was accompanied by the partition of India. It was an unprecedented human crisis. During the tumultuous period, the civil servants, mostly Indians (the British officials had either left or were in the process of winding up their personal assets) worked around the clock to look after the refugees, settling them or rescuing their family members, especially women and old men. Their dedication and their competence won the confidence of the founders of modern India.

Before independence, the civil servants were considered just an ally of the colonial power and an instrument of repression, but the mist against them disappeared during the post-1947 years. The unprecedented challenges and human tragedy enabled the civil services to establish their credentials before the new regime. With the departure of the colonial masters, the country masters had to learn the art of self- governance. The founders of modern India, Jawaharlal Nehru, the first Prime Minister and Sardar Vallabhai Patel, the Home Minister, realized that India needs competent and devoted volunteers to modernize the colonial systems to responsive democratic polity. They realized, appreciated, and now harnessed and assigned the civil servants, once considered the steel- frame of the colonial power in India, to evolve a stable political administrative system to be responsive and cater to the needs of the changing aspirations of the common people. The closest Advisors to the Ministers were these very civil servants of the Indian Civil Service, the ICS. Sardar Patel successfully persuaded the heads of the Provincial Governments and got their consent to the continuation of the steel-frame to serve the motherland.

New nomenclatures were given to the civil and police services with the Indian Administrative Services and the Indian Police Service replacing the ICS and IP. The founders of the Constitution decided to protect the officials of the existing civil services as well as the new All India Services from partisan politics.

In USA, the conflict between the political establishment and the bureaucracy continues to haunt even in the 21st century. It was much pronounced, when two civil women officials gave evidence before the Senate during the impeachment of the President, Donald Trump. They were later sacked and accused of being partisan against the president.

In India, during the elections and also at various levels, the civil servants could express their neutral opinion. The election commissioners, the officials of the investigating agencies, come in frequent conflict with the powers that be, face the wrath of the political masters, but are seldom sacked.

The All India Services, and the former Indian Civil Service officers, manned not only the offices of the Central Government but all the important posts in the provinces. It was through these officers that the Union Government, which was the regulating authority of these All India Services, and the ICS, could function without hassle. The Indian constitution has well-defined the powers of the states/ provinces and the Union. The civil services, well versed in the constitutional laws and their respective role within the system, could function even during the challenging periods. The lock-down of a country, with almost 1.3 billion people, could be achieved due to the key-role of the civil services, amidst the pandemic of Covid-19. Like their predecessors, they too worked with dedication, and received appreciation in the country's key newspapers and television channels.

In the recruitment of civil servants in India after Independence, the concept of the generalist administrator was strongly stressed. It also promoted the concept of an ideal administrator having a macro approach with micro details, an all-rounder, who could be moved from one job to another with zeal to make each sector successful. He was expected to be capable of taking a practical, non-partisan view on any issue. The challenging experience they gain in the district under the state administration, helps an Indian civil service official to serve, supervise and manage the vast structure of bureaucracy of the Union with rare in-depth understanding. Their counterparts in USA, do not have such multi-layer experiences.

Under the Government of India Act of 1935, elections were held. It had introduced a federal form of Government, with the provinces enjoying autonomy in their functions. A paradigm change in the functioning of the services took place with the eected ministers in the saddle of the provincial government. The officials were expected to serve the new political bosses having the people's mandate, while being loyal to his Majesty's government. Indeed, it was a tight-rope walking, but with the World War-II in 1939, the process of transforming the civil services of the colonial masters to serve their motherland was stalled for a few years. The Viceroy declared the participation of India in the war without consulting the provincial governments. The popular ministries in all the provinces resigned and the provinces came directly under the British appointed Governors in the nine provinces. The services were now asked to make war-efforts. It changed the focus of administration range during the war years, 1939-45.

The term All India Services was first used in 1898. Together with the Imperial Civil Service (ICS) a number of other Central Services were also set up from time to time to cater to the expanding role of the government. From the nineteen twenties till the time of Independence,

Civil Services stood classified as follows:

All India Services

- The Imperial (Indian) Civil Services
- The Indian Police (IP) Service
- The Indian Forest Service
- The Indian Education Service

Central Civil Services: Reporting to the Viceroy and the Central Government.

Provincial Services: Reporting to the Government of the State

Subordinate Services

The British ensured that the Imperial Civil Service i.e. the ICS, became an elite service to man all the important administrative positions, both at the Centre and in Provinces. Under the colonial administration, the role of the Civil Service was both of policy making as well as execution of policies. As mentioned earlier, there were no elected ministers in the provinces till 1935. The Central Assembly, under provisions of Government of India Act 1921, comprised officials as well as elected members. The All India Services were under the Secretary of State for India in London. They were accountable to the colonial power (but we must not forget that even under the British Rule, the civil servants were working under a democratic regime). The Secretary of State for India was a member of the British cabinet, elected by the voters in UK. The

House of Commons known as the mother of all elected bodies in the world, came into being under the strong British traditions, though functioning under an unwritten constitution. The Indian affairs and actions of the civil servants were discussed and scrutinized in the British Parliament.

During the colonial administration, the new civil and criminal legal systems replaced the different laws or tradition adopted in the administration of justice in various parts of the country. The Indian Penal Code, the Indian Evidence Act and the Criminal Procedure Code were introduced during this period. The young ICS officials were expected to learn these legal provisions and had to function in conformity with these new legal entities.

Apart from the administrative work, the ICS officers were also functioning as judicial officers adjudicating cases. In absence of elected representatives, they had acquired an image of a benevolent functionary of the crown. For the subjects in the British India, he was venerated as a "guardian" or mai-baap looking after their welfare. The professional administration brought peace and tranquility in the countryside. There was anarchy and lawlessness in the country before the British authority was firmly entrenched. With the decline of the Mughals in Delhi and assertion of the Mughal subedars (governors) as sovereign rulers in various parts of India from Bengal, Oudh, Hyderabad and even in Kabul, anarchy had griped the country. The civil services reintroduced systems and ensured peace in the country. It received admiration from the common people.

The country's connectivity improved with the construction of the railway lines and installation of telegraph lines. Within India, people could travel easily, and the setting up of the government schools and universities, exposed them to the western education and English language. This interaction with the West ushered in a renaissance in India. There was a growing realization about the prevailing inadequacies, and a close-minded approach in the Indian society. Reformers like Raja Ram Mohan Roy challenged the outdated customs like Sati (immolation of widows) and Sir Syed Ahmad Khan established the Anglo Mohammedan College at Aligarh in UP to end the apathy among the Muslims, who had faced unprecedented repression following the failure of the 1857 uprising. The western education complemented the efforts of Indians, who were keen for self-rule under the British Empire. There was a growing demand for more and more Indian presence in the ICS. The service, was initially conceived to only serve the colonial power, but its talented officials earned respect and prestige across India. Even after the appointment of separate judicial officers as judges in the subordinate courts as well as in the high courts, the ICS were assigned quasi-judicial responsibilities. This practice continues even today in various tribunals of the Union and the state governments.

The ICS was a close-knit service, designed primarily for maintenance of law and order and collection of revenue, but over the years they became multi-task officials. These officials were not responsible to the people whom they ruled, but their personal character and ethics earned them respect, accompanied by the awe of the power they wielded. The officials were often accused of being paternalistic, too much rigid and they could not redress the problems at the grassroots, nor did they come to grips with the political, economic and social problems of the masses. They were firm believers of status quo, but not oriented towards development. However, the officials could complement in the formation of policies, but the decision had to come from the elected leaders. Even in contemporary India, the Zamindari abolition and various land reforms could take place due to the effective role of the civil services. The transparency in the administrative system could effectively be introduced by the Right to Information Act 2005. It replaced the draconian law of the Official Secrets Act of 1923, which had prevented the people from known facts about any decision taken in the government files. The character and commitment of the old civil service is being retained even today. The District Magistrate, who controls both the police and the revenue administration, continues to command respect.

Interim Government and Role of the Civil Service

With the enactment of the India Independence Act 1947, the two Dominions of India and Pakistan came into existence. The Civil servants as well as the military officers were given the options to stay back in India or join the new Government in Pakistan. The India (Provisional Constitution) Order 1947 introduced certain structural changes in the constitution of the civil services in India. The essence of this change was the transfer of control from the Secretary of State sitting in UK to the Governor of the State in so far as affairs of the provinces were concerned.

An Interim Government was formed under Jawaharlal Nehru, pending the adoption of a new Constitution. With Partition and Independence, the three most urgent tasks of administration were;

- Restoration of peace and confidence building in the citizens.
- Devising strategies to persuade the 560 odd princes, rulers to join the Indian Dominion.
- Gearing administration towards democracy and aiming at establishing a secular, socialist society for ensuring equity and justice to all.

These tasks involved new enlarged responsibilities for the administration which has to acquire skills for assessing the people's needs, involving people's participation and ensuring that development policies and programmes reached the target group.

The ordeal of the partition, that followed Independence, brought an exodus of refugees in very large numbers. It was a human tragedy following the polarization of the people in the name of religion. The neighbours, living as brothers for generations, became blood-thirsty of each other, if one of them either was a Hindu or Muslim.

It has been seen worldwide that violence is mostly caused by misinformation and for political reasons. India was no exception. There are still boundary walls dividing the Roman Catholics and Protestants in Northern Ireland. In contemporary USA, the race violence has shocked people worldwide, though the man who killed the black belonged to the same religion, Christianity. In Pakistan, which was carved out from British India, to provide a Muslim homeland, the majority Sunnis were victimized and decimated in its eastern wing, because they were Bengalis. It had led to the formation of Bangladesh. In the remaining Pakistan, in spite of following the same religion, Shias are being frequently killed and Ahmedias have been declared non-Muslims.

With these much-pronounced social, religious and ethnic varieties, the challenges before the civil servants become formidable, if not impossible. It is difficult even to imagine today how the civil society was restrained from being too violent; it was a traumatic experience even for those who tried to rescue people amidst dead bodies, restoring their children and women. The Indian officials did it. It was an experience unbelievable for the contemporary Indians. Massive rescue and rehabilitation took place, when more than half of the senior officers of the ICS, mostly British, had left the country. In spite of thinning of its strength, the truncated civil service rose to the occasion. It took up the challenge with courage, endurance and imaginative efforts. They looked after the relief and rehabilitation of the refugees and administered the rationing system which became necessary due to the shortage in the post-World War-II environment. It was mainly due to the remarkable performances of the Civil Services in that period, that the country was saved from catastrophe.

The challenges before the nascent Indian state, as an independent nation, continued to haunt during the post-independent period. Partition was followed by an unprecedented migration of population, intermittent violence, the integration of the princely states, integration of the tribal people into the mainstream of national life, and the problems of the North-East. The north-east region, the sub-Himalayan areas comprising the present day, Mizoram, Nagaland, Manipur, Arunachal Pradesh and Meghalaya were the abode of variety of tribes having distinct ethnic identities. These areas were always put under the direct supervision of the Governor General. The entry to these areas was restricted and forbidden. The British had encouraged their conversion to a particular sect of Christianity (Methodist and Protestant) and they were kept in isolation. They were also told that they do not belong to the mainland India. The Naga and Mizo insurgencies received liberal assistance from Pakistan and China. They could be brought to the main stream of India only after the formation of Bangladesh. Interesting, it may be noted that British, though keen to have an independent Crown Colony, did not support the insurgencies, but the USA's intelligence agency, CIA, was helping their leaders with resources and access to political leaders of Europe and USA.

The civil services served all the sections, in spite of financial constraints. In the life of a nation, particularly a developing country like India, surviving with her glorious civilization, retaining all-inclusive traditions, though defaced during a 250-year of colonial subjugation survival as a united country, itself was a formidable challenge. However, India with her systems, manned by an accomplished bureaucracy, wading through complex social structures, a vibrant democracy with civil liberties and free press could survive. Amidst challenges, several shocks and upheavals, the country has asserted itself as a stable polity, that too under a strong well-entrenched democratic system. The bureaucracy assiduously carried out remedial tasks laid down by the Indian constitution and the Government. This period, witnessed the graduation of the colonial civil service, an instrument of subjugation, to become an instrument for retaining democracy, fair governance and rule of law.

The new political leaders, the veteran freedom fighters, provided political stability, but were not well-versed in the intricacies of the governance. In this environment, the role of the Civil Services became crucial to keep the nation secured. This period also witnessed the first Indo Pakistan war over Kashmir and the successful integration to India, of more than 500 princely States and principalities.

The Constitution of India was adopted on 26th June 1950, and the elected Governments, both in the Centre and the States came into existence in 1952, with the elections held under the new Constitution. The new factor that emerged after independence was the emergence of the Indian politician as an effective ruler under the

Cabinet system of administration. The civil servants at the top of the administrative system, no longer acted as representatives of the English crown, but had to act under, and were responsible to the Indian Minister in-charge of the Department.

However, India's leading statesmen like Jawaharlal Nehru and Sardar Patel, did not want to change the position of members of the Indian Civil Service in any way and they were guaranteed a number of privileges. However, the exercise of political power by Ministers and later on by legislators, eroded gradually, the privileged position of the top civil servants and they had to learn more and more the art of management of their political masters.

Constitutional Protection for Civil Servants

In part XIV of the Constitution of India, a separate Chapter for the Civil Services was included. These were Articles 309, 310, 311, 312 and 312A. The Article 309 details about the recruitment and conditions of service of persons serving the Union or State. It authorized the appropriate Legislature to make Acts to regulate the recruitment, and conditions of service of persons appointed, to public services and post in connection with the affairs of the Union or of any State.

Article 310 lays down the rules regarding the tenure of persons who are in the defence service, or of a civil service of the Union or of an all India service or holds any post connected with defence or any civil post under the

Union holds office during the pleasure of the President, and every person who is member of a civil service of a State or holds any civil post under State holds office during the pleasure of the Governor of the State. Article 311 states that no person who is a member of a civil service of the Union or an All India Service or a civil service of a State or holds a civil post under the Union or a State shall be dismissed or removed by an authority subordinate to that by which he was appointed. Sub section 2 of this Article further states that dismissal or removal or reduction in rank can take place only after an inquiry in which he is informed of the charges against him and he has given reasonable opportunity of being heard in respect of those charges. Article 312 empowers the Council of States to create one or more All India Services apart from the Indian Administrative Service and the Indian Police Service which were existing prior to the commencement of the Constitution.

It may also be mentioned here that the Constitution further provided in Article 315 and 320 that there shall be a separate Public Service Commission of the Union and a Public Service Commission in each state, which shall conduct examinations for appointments to the services of the Union and the States respectively. It will also be consulted on all matters of recruitment to civil services and civil posts and all disciplinary matters.

❑

CHAPTER 2

Historical Evolution of Bureaucracy in USA

During the period when India was being subjugated in the seventeenth and eighteenth centuries, the settlers in America, mostly migrants of the British Isles and some Europeans, were becoming restless. They were convinced that the authorities in England had no business to regulate or rule them. The settlers, who were spread in the vast American lands, had declared themselves as 13 independent countries. They knew that if they do not work out a basic law for binding them together, they might soon lose their newly acquired freedom. They therefore decided to federate as the United States of America. They framed a federal constitution on September 17, 1787, but retained their separate State constitutions. It enabled them to retain their respective autonomy, while transforming some powers to the Federal Government.

The leaders of the 13 states were aware of the presence of many among them continuing to have allegiance to the

British King. They realized their inadequacy in dealing with the British forces and the need to consolidate their newly acquired independence by forming a viable federation. The delegates to the Constitutional Convention sought a stronger, more viable federal union, but they were also intent on safeguarding the existing self-governance enjoyed of the States.

Even prior to the formation of State, these existed the governments of the counties and smaller units. This was because one of the first tasks accomplished by the English settlers was the creation of governmental units for the tiny settlements they established among the Atlantic coast. And as the new settlers pushed westwards, each frontier outpost created its own local government to manage its affairs.

The framers of the US Constitution, quite intelligently allowed these multi layered governmental systems untouched. They made the national structure sovereign, but wisely recognized these autonomous state self-governed institutions necessary for the newly evolved federation.

The people of these States had refused the colonial administration of London. It was, therefore not possible to accept another repressive regimen even within a federal framework. The governments in the states and the counties within the States were directly in contact with the people and more keenly attuned to their needs. They recognized that certain functions such as defence, currency regulation and foreign relations could only be managed by a strong

Federal Government, but other functions such as sanitation, education and local transportation could be better served by local jurisdictions.

In India, the Constitution demarcates the powers of the Union and the States in three lists, but the Concurrent List empowers the Union to legislate, which reduces the role of the States. But in USA, the federal Government could function only within the jurisdictions marked for it. In general matters that lie entirely within state borders are the exclusive concerns of the State governments. These include internal communications, regulations relating to property, industry, business and public utilities. The state criminal code and working conditions within the State.

However, with the expansion of the economy, the functioning or role of the federal initiatives often overlap with state jurisdictions. In recent years, the federal government has assumed ever broadening responsibility in such matters as health, education, welfare, transportation, housing and urban development. But where the federal government exercises such responsibilities in the states, programs are usually adopted on the basis of cooperation between two levels of governments, rather than as an imposition from above.

The founders of the US constitution did not consider the need for a permanent civil service for manning the federal government.

The second paragraph of Section 2 of Article 11 of the US Constitution states as follows:

He (the President) shall have power, by and with the advice and consent of the Senate, to make treaties, provided two thirds of the Senators present concur; and shall nominate, and by and with the advice and consent of the Senate, shall appoint ambassadors, other public ministers and consuls, judges of the Supreme Court, and all other officers of the United States, whose appointments are not herein otherwise provided for, and which shall be established by law but the Congress may be law vest the appointment of such inferior (subordinate) officers, as they think proper, in the President alone, in the courts of law, or in the heads of departments. The President shall have power to fill up all vacancies that may happen during recess of the senate, by granting Commissions which shall expire at the end of their next session.

The Section 4 of the same Article says, "The President, Vice President and all civil officers of the United States, shall be removed from office on impeachment for, and conviction of, treason, bribery, or other high crimes and misdemeanours".

The spoil system of the appointment of the factors or officials under the EIC in India was also followed in the newly constituted federation of the United States. In the early 19th century, positions in the Federal Government were held at the pleasure of the President. A person could be fired at any time. What was prevalent was the Spoils

System. The Spoils System meant that jobs were used to support the American political parties. The result was that as long as a particular President was in office, he had supporters in all offices and they did all they could that the President belonging to their own party was elected or reelected. The work of the Government was conducted on partisan-lines. If their party was overthrown in the next election, they all had to get out and the new President put his own followers in those positions.

There was rampant corruption in the US system. The corruption was accompanied by inefficiency and irresponsibility. The experienced and worthy public officials were ousted to make room for the new President's political henchmen. The public services got demoralized every time a change of administration took place. It was also quite a challenging task for the new President to accommodate his supporters and party. The President was harassed almost beyond endurance by place seekers and their friends. The congressmen tended to become more solicitous and dispensers of patronage. Their favouritism resembled the conduct of the London-based directors of the EIC, offering plum positions to their favourites in India. While the number of the EIC directors used to be about 30-35, the Congressmen were much more in numbers. Their focus was on getting their favourites appointed in the federal system, instead of legislating federal laws.

It was soon realized that the administration based on the prevailing spoil system was becoming politically counter-productive. The prestige of the politicians in the

USA had declined due to the non-performing officials. The administration fell to low-level, politics itself grew mercenary and corrupt. There was a demand to put an end to this system, especially after one of the Presidents, James Garfield was mortally wounded by a deranged President was preparing to board a train in Washington (July 2nd, 1881).

The Congress enacted the Pendleton Civil Service Reform Act in 1883. It led to the formation of the United States Civil Service Commission. Its function was to supervise and administer the Civil Service of the Federal Government. It introduced the competitive examinations to ensure the selection of the federal government employees on the basis of merit. It served the twin purpose of protecting the tenure of the civil servants even after the change in the administration in the elections and also insulated the civil servants from the influences of political patronage and partisan behaviour. This system of ending appointment of the political favourites in the civic bodies and the state administration could not percolate down to the local administration.

The Congressmen became unhappy with the implementation of the Pendleton Act. It had adversely affected their power of patronage and influence in the administrative system. After two years, the law makers stopped the funding of this Commission, but they had to relent following the countrywide outrage on this issue. Under the public pressure, the funding was restored. The impact of this merit-based appointment system was quite deep. Almost two thirds of the US Federal workforce was appointed on the basis of merit by 1909. The qualifications of the aspirants for the federal jobs were measured by open tests. However, certain senior level positions, including some heads of diplomatic missions and executive agencies, continued to be filled with political appointments.

In a bid to ensure non-partisan role of the civil servants, they were debarred from engaging in political activities under the Hatch Act 1939. It ensured security of job to the employees, but in some cases the legal provisions of the job protection were invoked by an out-going administration to ensure job security to its political appointees. This is called "burrowing" in civil service jargon. The commission was renamed as the Office of Personnel Management on January 1, 1978. It was done under the provisions of Reorganization Plan number 2 of 1978 and the Civil Service Reform Act of 1978. The Civil Service Reform Act of 1978 created the US office of Personnel Management and the Merit Systems Protection Board. In addition, namely other functions were placed under the Equal Opportunity Commission namely the Federal Labour Relations Authority and the Office of Special Counsel.

Civil service reform represents one of the earliest attempts to "rationalize" local administration by instituting a system of written examinations for municipal appointees and by insulating administrative personnel from political influence through tenure (White, 1949; Griffith, 1974). This entailed legally investing responsibility for personnel appointments in a central agency or commission. For the most part, civil service procedures were not required by law or other regulations. The only piece of national civil service legislation during this period, the Pendleton Act of 1882, dealt exclusively with federal government organizations and did not mention local or state government (Thelen, 1972). It was also a relatively "weak law that effectively allowed each administration to classify public offices as it chose" (Wiebe, 1967: 61). Only three states - New York, Massachusetts, and Ohio- adopted state-wide measures for civil service reform during the time period considered here. Most city governments were not required to adopt civil service reform because they were relatively autonomous of higher-level organizations, state or federal (Griffith, 1974; Gelfand, 1975).

With growth of the Progressive Movement, and its emphasis on scientific management (Griffith, 1974: 15), came a basis for government reform. Basically, the reform movement attempted to change the conception of the city from that of a political body to that of a business corporation, with the city "a joint stock affair in which the taxpayers are the stockholders" (Clinton, 1886; Crandon, 1886-1887: 524). Reformers engaged in a series of highly publicized struggles to promote municipal reforms in almost every major city (Wiebe, 1967: 168). The first city passed legislation requiring civil service in 1884; by 1935, over 450 cities across the United States had enacted some type of civil service legislation (Van Riper, 1951). Thus, by 1935 the transformation of a city government from a politically based system to a bureaucratically based system was well underway (Hays, 1972: 9).

City Governments

Once predominantly rural, the United States is today a highly urbanized country, and about 80 percent of its citizens now live in towns, large cities, or suburbs of cities. The statistics reveal that the city governments play a critically important role in the system of governance. The City governments are chartered by States, and their charters detail the objectives and powers of the municipal government, but in many respects the cities enjoy autonomy. In India too, the local bodies were empowered through two constitutional amendments, 73rd and 74th but the states are reluctant to shed off their centralized power. These amendments in India provide autonomy to the local bodies from the district level to the village-level.

In USA, the systems in the city governments vary widely across the nation. However, almost all have some kind of central council, elected by the voters, and an Executive Officer, assisted by various departmental heads. They jointly manage the city's affairs. There are three types of city governments; the Mayor Council, the Commission and the City Manager. In the first one, an elected Mayor and an elected Council function together. The Mayor appoints heads of city departments and other officials. In the second case, the legislative and executive functions in one group of officials, usually three or more in number elected city wide. In the third system, the city manager holds most of the executive powers, including law enforcement and provision of services. It is entrusted to a highly trained and experienced professional city manager. The city manager is paid administrator. The manager draws up the city budget and supervises most of the departments. Usually there is no set tenure, the manager serves as long as the council is satisfied with his or her work. Its functioning resembles the urban development authorities in India. The only difference is that the urban authorities are appointed by the state governments, but in US, they are appointed and accountable to the city council.

In most US countries, one town or city is designated as the county seat, and this is where the government offices are located. The board levies taxes, borrows and appropriates money; fixes the salaries of county employees and administers national, state and county welfare programmes.

Town and Village Government

There are thousands of municipal jurisdictions, but they are too small to qualify as city governments. They are chartered as towns and villages and deal with such strictly local needs as paving and lighting the street ensuring water supply, providing police and fire protection, establishing local health regulations, arranging for garbage, sewage, and other waste disposal, collecting local taxes etc. Governmental employees may include a clerk, treasurer, police and fire officers, and health and welfare officers. It may be noted that the people volunteer in managing the services like fire brigade. They are trained by fire brigade officers and they are not employees. They participate in saving precious life during fire incidents or any other calamity. The US Bureau of the Census has identified no less than 84,955 local governmental units in the US including counties, municipalities, townships, school districts and special districts.

State Executives

The State executive consists of a Governor, a Lieutenant Governor, a Secretary of State, an Attorney General, an Auditor, a Treasurer, Superintendents, etc. In the Federal Government there are four general type divisions: Cabinet Departments, Independent Executive Agencies, Regulatory Agencies and Government corporations.

There are currently fifteen Cabinet Departments in the Federal government. Cabinet departments are major executive offices that are directly accountable to the President. They include the Departments of State, Defence, Education, Treasury and several others. A department is abolished, when its tasks no longer need direct presidential and congressional oversight, such as happened to the Post Office Department in 1970. Each Cabinet department has a head called a Secretary, appointed by the President and confirmed by the Senate. These Secretaries, who are political appointees, report directly to the President, and they oversee a huge network of offices and agencies that make up the department. They also work in different capacities to achieve each department's mission-oriented functions. Within these large bureaucratic networks are a number of undersecretaries, assistant Secretaries, deputy secretaries and many others. The Department of Justice is the one department that is structured differently. Rather than a Secretary and under Secretary, it has an Attorney General, an associate general and a host of different bureau and division heads.

The fifteen Departments are State, Treasury, Justice, Interior, Agriculture, Commerce, Labour, Defence, Health and Human Services, Housing and Urban Development, Transportation, Energy, Education, Veterans Affairs; Homeland Security. Each cabinet department comprises multi-layer subordinate bureaucracy. These levels descend from the departmental heads in a most hierarchical pattern and consist of essential staff, smaller offices and bureaus. These hierarchical structures allow deployment of a large number of officials dedicated to address many different subjects and specialized officers. For example, below the Secretary of State, are a number of Undersecretaries. These include undersecretaries for political affairs, for management, for economic growth, energy and the environment, and many others. Each controls a number of bureaus and offices. Each bureau and office in turn oversees more focused aspects of the Under Secretaries field of specialization. For example, below the undersecretary for public diplomacy and public affairs are three bureaus; education and cultural affairs, public affairs and international information programme. Frequently, these bureaus have even more specialized departments under them. Under the bureau of Educational and Cultural

Affairs are spokesman for the Department of State and his or her staff, the Office of the Historian and the United States Diplomacy Centre.

Independent Executive Agencies and Regulatory Agencies

Like cabinet departments, independent executive agencies report directly to the President, with heads appointed by the President. Unlike the larger Cabinet Departments however, independent agencies are assigned far more focused tasks. These agencies are considered independent because they are not subject to the regulatory authority of any specific department. They perform vital functions and are a major part of the bureaucratic landscape of the United States providing information or services. Some prominent agencies are the Central Intelligence Agency, which collects and manages intelligence vital to national interests and the National Aeronautics and Space Administration (NASA) charged with developing technological innovation for the purpose of space exploration.

The independent regulatory agency systems emerged in the late nineteenth century as a product of the push to control the benefits and costs of industrialization. The first Regulatory Agency was the Interstate Commerce Commission, charged with regulating that most identifiable and prominent symbol of industrialization, the railroad. Other Regulatory agencies such as the Commodity Futures Trading Commission, which regulates US Financial markets and the Federal Communications Commission, which regulates radio and Television have largely been created in the image of the ICC. The Securities and Exchange Commission (SEC) illustrates the key role and the power, these agencies have in their respective fields. The SEC's mission has expanded significantly in the digital era beyond mere regulation of stock floor trading.

Government Corporations

Agencies formed by the federal government to administer a quasi-business enterprise are called government corporations. They exist because the services they provide are partly subject to market forces, and tend to generate enough profit to be self-sustaining, but they also fulfil a vital service, the government has an interest in maintaining. Unlike a private corporation, a government corporation has no stakeholders. Instead it has a board of Directors and managers. These government-owned corporations are exempt from taxes.

❑

CHAPTER 3

Historical Evolution of Bureaucracy in China

After having gone in some depth on the evolution of bureaucracies in two of the strongest and most populous democracies in the world, it is of utmost importance to study the evolution of the bureaucracy/civil service in China, the economic powerhouse of the world, only next to the USA. China can rightly be called the leader of the Communist countries, as Russia has lost its sheen after it broke up under Gorbachev.

The People's Republic of China, with a population of 1.4 billion, was founded in 1949. It is a unitary State, with a small but powerful Central Government, that presides over 30 provinces. In 1996, the provinces were organized into 334 prefectures, which in turn were organized into 2142 counties and 640 municipalities. Counties were further subdivided into districts (State Statistical Bureau 1996). A unified, national civil service was organized throughout the country.

For most of the past 70 years, China has known only a public (or collective) sector (there was no private sector) in which virtually all urban employees have been public employees (Burns and Bidhya Bowornwathana). As mentioned in the study quoted in the book "Civil Services System in Asia" (2001), the number of selected public employees in the Peoples Republic of China in 1996 were at least 80 million people or about 6.7% of the total population comprising officials and staff of the Government Agencies, Civil Servants, Party Agencies, Railroads, Posts and Telecommunications, Health care, Education, Public utilities and Public enterprises.

The first official definition of civil servants was given in 1993 in China. Civil Servants, numbering 5.285 million cadres, were defined to be those administrators, managers and professionals who work for government agencies. A separate management system was established for them. China's official civil service is both more exclusive and more inclusive than found in other countries. Excluded from the civil service are all blue-collar workers regardless of whether they work for government agencies. China's preference for separate management regimes for white and blue-collar workers reflects the Chinese perception that mental and manual workers make different contributions to the value of production. This is also part of China's historical legacy.

Historical Evolution of the Chinese Civil Services

Imperial China produced the 'world's educated bureaucracy chosen fundamentally on the basis of merit. The imperial system, characterized by selection of the meritorious, based on examinations, was already its zenith during the Song dynasty (960-1126). This was one of the greatest achievements of the Chinese civilization.

Since democracy needs a permanent system i.e. civil service like it existed in India, but it was fine tuned in China, with a system of electing higher officials on the basis of merit. However, like India, China too faced the European invaders, especially EIC. The beautifully nurtured system collapsed by the twentieth century because of foreign aggression and rampant corruption. The last imperial civil service examination was held in 1904.

In 1911, a Revolution took place and a Republican Government came to power. Reformers like Sun Yatsen tried to combine the civil service reforms being pursued in the Western countries, with China's own traditions of competitive literati examinations. By the mid-twenties, efforts to reform the civil service were well under way. The government functionaries began to be referred as administrative personnel. In 1933, the State formally referred to government functionaries as public servants in the Law on the Appointment of Public Servants. They were no longer called "officials".

During the successive Republican era constitutions (1912-1949), the civil servants were to be selected, based on competitive examinations and were to be responsible to the people, through elected legislature. Though provisions existed to protect the civil servants from political pressure or arbitrary dismissal, these provisions were not always employed in practice. Discharge of public servants frequently occurred, not only on political grounds but also for personal reasons. In 1916, the first higher level civil service examinations were held (first after 1905). Attempts were made to establish a neutral and professional civil service in China. In 1930, the Examination Yuan was established and in 1931 biannual higher-level civil service examinations were introduced.

It is significant to note however that apart from testing knowledge of classical Chinese and technical competence, loyalty to the Nationalist Party/ State was also required. In 1932, the Ministry of Personnel was established to manage the civil service as a whole. It established uniform pay scales and retirement benefits for all civil servants.

Eligibility for appointment included: passing the examination, graduating from University, graduating from an upper level specialised school, 'serving the Nationalist revolution' over a period of years, or incumbency in a government position. The recommendations of the Yuan Examination were in the initial years seen as unwarranted interference but after some years, more and more appointees had Examination Yuan credentials. By 1940, even the Nationalist Party was forwarding the credentials of its incumbents to the Ministry of Personnel for approval. Thus, the Ministry helped to 'build and maintain the status of the upper civil service as a prestigious profession based on merit-based appointments. In spite of these gains, the official personnel system never provided more than 1% of the civil service as a whole.

In 1937, Japan invaded China. Concerned about its control, the Nationalist Party reoriented the civil service examinations away from professional competence toward ensuring political responsiveness and loyalty to the Party. To this end, those who passed the civil service examination were required to under as six to nine month long training courses run by the Nationalist Party School before they were permitted to take another examination that qualified them for the coveted appointment. Ideology in the examination process was paralleled by a series of "training classes" for civil servants already on the job. Through it the party sought to indoctrinate and standardize the thoughts and values of those in the civil service.

To meet the needs of the expanding civil service, recruitment through informal mechanisms and personal relations network become more and more important. The civil war with the Chinese Communist Party (CCP) and its People's Liberation Army (PLA), that broke out at the end of the Second World War only intensified these trends and undermined further institutionalization of processes for managing the civil services (John P. Burns).

In 1949, the People's Republic of China was founded. The CCP referred to its functionaries by the generic term "cadres". This included party workers, Government officials or the Army. In this usage, cadre referred to those who had a certain level of education, who had some special ability and who carried out "mental" rather than "manual" labour.

❑

CHAPTER 4

Role of the Civil Services in India

The objectives of governance were clearly laid down in the Preamble to the Constitution of India adopted on 26th January 1950. It states, "WE, THE PEOPLE OF INDIA, having solemnly resolved to constitute India into a SOVEREIGN SOCIALIST SECULAR DEMOCRATIC REPUBLIC and to secure to all its citizens:

JUSTICE social economic and political;

LIBERTY of thought expression belief faith and worship;

EQUALITY of status and of opportunity;

And to promote among them all

FRATERNITY assuring the dignity of the individual and the unity and integrity of the nation

It is this philosophy that permeates the entire civil services in India.

The civil service system in post independent India was reorganized. At the Central level, the civil services include the All India services such as the IAS, the Indian Foreign Service and the Indian police service, and the central services. The Central Services were grouped into four categories. The union territories were to be served both by the All India and Central Services. The various provinces of the country had to have their own Services.

The difference between the US civil services and the Indian civil services was that USA has no all-American civil services like the IAS. USA has a separate federal service and the States have separate civil services. There has been little attempt to enable the federal services to be exposed to the local administration. It was perhaps this reason, why President Johnson's initiative to uplift the poor, could not be delivered the desired results. The federal officials did not have much understanding about reaching the poor and the disadvantages sections. On the other hand, most of the top officials in the Union Government in India have served the districts.

The founders of modern India realized that unless the states take initiative in economic emancipation of the common people that development of the country cannot take place. During the colonial rule the self-sustained agriculture, had become non -productive. The farmers were exploited and had to cough up land rent through a repressive zamindari system. The cottage industry was destroyed for providing the British industrial products. The rough cloth manufactured in the huge Manchester textile mills were given tax incentives at the cost of the fine textiles weaved in India. India was the captive market for the finished product of the industrialized world. Also, India did not have any capitalists, except the house of the Tatas; there was just traders, but no entrepreneurs. A few factories were set up during the World War-I and World War-II, but no large scale industrial activity took place in British India.

India's all-round progress began with the economic planning in India in 1951, with the launch of its five year plan, which enjoined on the Indian civil service the role of development administration. In this new mould they were expected to participate in the administration of public enterprises, regulations of the private sector, formulation of the socio-economic and political policies, elimination of poverty, development of rural areas, the fight against inflation, effective monetary management, reduction of the gender gap, elimination of social inequity etc. In the initial years, the role of the civil servant was to guide India's planned development to build up, by democratic means, a rapidly expanding and technological progress economy and technologically progressive economy and a social order based on equality and justice.

During the First Five Year plan, an institutional structure for integrated rural development through community development block started in 1952. The main function of civil service was to ensure that through the development blocks, scientific and technical knowledge, animal husbandry and rural industry was passed on to the rural population. Establishment of the national extension programme was the first reform since independence for decentralized development.

The second Five Year Plan and stressed the need for creating within each district, a well-organized democratic structure of administration in which the village panchayats would be organically linked with elected organisation at a higher level, but the state politics prevented the growth of the civic bodies. A large number of the civic bodies was superseded and administrators were appointed, who would be serving the interest of the powers-that-be in the state government. However, there was a proliferation of officials at various level. The successive governments ignored the British norms of keeping the administrative cost low. The administration had become so heavy that the most of the budget for the development was spent in paying salaries.

The District Collector, District Development officers and the Block Development officer became the key officers to co-ordinate the activities of different development officers at the district and block levels. The civil services were expected to ensure that the basic goals of development as laid down in the Five-Year Plans were achieved. The basic objectives were to improve the economic conditions of the weaker section, increasing employment opportunities and providing basic needs to the people, like clean drinking water, provisions of medical and health services, spread of primary education, linking of villagers with all-weather roads etc. During the successive Five-Year Plan food self-sufficiency was achieved. India also become one of the leading producers of milk in the world. Industrialization took place, but it was mostly in the government sectors. Private capital was not encouraged.

However, the political establishment during the first decade of planning started changing. The committed freedom fighters, who were the political bosses during the initial years, were being replaced by the new crop of politicians. They were hungry for power. The country's political parties needed his funds to win elections. The parties, which could not receive more points started promoting sectarian politics to win votes. Yet the Indian democracy has survived.

In the name of promoting smaller industries, the MRTP (Monopolies Trade Restrict Practices) was introduced. The 1956 industrial Policy Resolution reserve the core sector to the public sector i.e. the government owned enterprises. The licensing system was introduced, which continued till the 1990s, when the economy was liberalized under the Prime Minister P. V. Narsimha Rao. Under the MRTP, a company will be fined, if it produced more cloth or shoes (then licensed). The ministers vied with each other to have a large number of public sector units. These industrial units suffered huge losses and the losses were to be compensated from the general budget.

The concept of the mixed economy was compromised due to inefficiency of the public sector. The recruitment in the civil services was on the basis of merit and success in the competitive examination. The public sector units with a few exceptions became the liability on the state exchequer.

Instead of providing level-playing opportunity to everyone, the licensing Raj promoted nexus between a section of the civil servants and the industrialists. Their political masters patronized them. The self-defeating narrow economic policies led to the country's stunted economic growth. It may be surprising to know that a large number of Indian entrepreneurs even migrated to China to set up their units. They found the industrial development environment much more investment friendly in China than in the open economy of India.

Because of rampant corruption, India was unable to invite or attract capital. The unnecessary debates, whether India should have a committed bureaucracy or whether civil services should be allowed to function for a larger cause continues to haunt India. The politicians often call for "committed bureaucrats" (as in USA).

The internal emergency was promulgated in 1976 following the High court verdict against the then Prime Minister Indira Gandhi. She was given an interim stay to file an appeal before the higher court, but the opposition demanded her resignation. With a view to crush this demand, emergency was proclaimed and important opposition leaders including Jayaprakash Narayan, Chandrashekhar and Chaudhary Charan Singh were arrested. Chandrashekhar and Chaudhary Charan Singh had served as the Prime Ministers for brief periods too. Press freedom was muzzled and draconian laws were imposed, even curtailing the powers of the judiciary. The civil servants were forced to follow illegal orders and massive arrests were made. That was the weakest hour of the civil servants.

The country's economic growth was stunted. The scholars of the top technical and engineering colleges such as IITs had to migrate to USA for jobs. Rhetoric had overtaken the administration. Economic growth during the period was called the Hindu Growth rate. In eighties, in an interview, LK Jha, a former ICS and governor of the Reserve Bank of India, even accused Jawaharlal Nehru of using the state instruments in the name of socialism and planned growth to usher in an era of controls and licenses. It dwarfed the Indian initiative, till Dr Manmohan Singh started dismantling the controls, which were only triggering off rampant corruption in governance.

This period also witnessed the initiation of a new campaign for "Garibi Hatao". The civil servants, both in the Planning Commission as well as the Ministries, evolved and formulated several programs for eradication of rural poverty e.g. DPAP (Drought Prone Area Program), SFDA (Small Farmer Development Agency), ICDP (Intensive Cattle Development Program), IAAP (Intensive Agriculture Area Program) etc.

While formulating the policies, the civil servants regretfully retained their elitist nature, and because of the initial distrust of people, there was a lack of communication between the administration and the masses. One reason for this, as enumerated by the economists, was the fact that the well-knit organized bureaucracy, preceded elected democracy in India.

The administration of these multifarious development programs, efficiently and economically, became the main concerns of the senior civil servants. Public administration became an instrument of social change. The civil servants were expected to have the capacity to forecast, project and understand the direction and tempo of major significant changes in the political and social environment: to plan for necessary or desirable changes; to adapt itself to changes demanded or planned by the political system and to innovate on its own.

As Lord Fulton of UK had earlier stated, it is not enough for a modern civil service to maintain status quo; it must innovate, and to innovate, it must have a "radar system" for scanning the future; it must be deeply involved in the social, economic, scientific and technological changes in the society around it. It must identify sufficiently in advance, the major problems likely to arise in the future and must work on them so that the political decisions which taken, might be as reasonable as possible.

All India services

To ensure an effective role for the Central Government in the administration of the country, one of the factors considered necessary was to have some acceptable and durable link between the State and the Central administration. After consultation with the States, the scheme of All India Services was accordingly made a part of the new constitution.

The role of the All India Service was to provide a very strong uniting link between the Centre and the States in the day-to-day administration of the country as these All India Services are common between the Centre and the States. The civil services provide uniform standards of administration from Kashmir in the North to Kanyakumari in the South, and from Gujarat in the West to West Bengal in the East.

The All India Services maintain close administrative links between the Centre and the States on a day-to-day basis. They ensure a coordinated and balanced socio-economic development of all the regions of the country as visualized in the Constitution. Though the officers of the All India Services are appointed by the President of India (i.e. the Central Government) their services are placed at the disposal of the States and they man all the top administrative posts in the State Government. They help to minimize centre-state tensions or points of friction.

The All India Services have played an effective role of making the federal polity a truly cooperative federation of the Centre and States. The role of the services was to bring the knowledge of the field to the Central Government and to bring to the State governments the policies and methods of the Central Government.

The role of the civil services has been of vital importance for the smooth transaction of day-to-day government business at the Centre and in the States. This has also been because of a spirit of camaraderie among the holders of higher-level posts in the States and under the Central

Government. Many issues of governance, usually get amicably settled, without assuming political dimensions or becoming matters of bitter dispute. The civil servants are usually able to arrive at pragmatic solutions at their own level within the politically approved frameworks. Political prejudices of one kind or the other do not come in way of understanding the view points and legitimate interest of the States.

The civil servant also plays the role of transferring expertise from one State to another. There had been several occasions in the past when IAS/ IPS officers from different State cadres had to be posted to Jammu and Kashmir, Assam, and Punjab etc. to strengthen administration of the State in tackling law and order situations.

> The Sarkaria Commission set up to view Centre State relation stated in paras 8.7.07 of its report.
>
> "We are convinced that these services are as much necessary today as they were when the Constitution was framed and continue to be one of the premier institutions for maintaining the unity of the country". Undoubtedly the members of the all India services have shown themselves capable of delivering the roles that the framers of the Constitution envisaged for them.

The Period: From 1991 to the Present Day

This period saw the opening up of the economy. Liberalization saw the end of several regulations and civil servants were now expected to positively promote growth with the help of the private sector. The Indian economy opened up to globalization and the civil servants were expected to play a lead role in international forums. The use of technology and e-governance was encouraged. Effective delivery of services was emphasized upon.

The role of the civil services is also determined by the relations between the political system and the bureaucratic system. The relation between the political system and bureaucratic system in a democracy has to be one of partnership. But since independence, this role has often been adversely affected and has become strained and dysfunctional in the development process. The relation between the bureaucracy and the people is also marked by the lack of harmony, and the ordinary people feel alienated from the civil servants. Yet people trust the civil servants and are keen to retain the system. Misbehaviour with any civil servant is frowned upon. A law maker in Delhi had misbehaved with some senior civil servants, that too before the Chief Minister. The Chief minister could not hush up the case, though the legislator belonged to his party, due to the public outrage. There was a demand that the person who committed the offence should be jailed immediately and must be prosecuted and convicted.

There are instances of conflicts between the political leaders and civil servants. Earlier, the political leaders wanted that the development process should be speeded up. They had suffered prolonged jail terms during the colonial era and wanted that the fruits of independence should percolate down to the common people. However, with the new generation of politicians, public life too is being used for making huge money. A number of politicians and bureaucrats have been jailed for indulging in corruption. These differences have aggravated due to the larger presence of legislators accused of committing crimes. They indulge in sectarian rhetoric to win elections and try to siphon of public money by conspiring with the corruption in the bureaucracy. The conflicts are being noticed at all the three levels, Centre, State and District.

A few of the political leaders want only their favourite tainted officials in their department. There is also some sort of understanding among the politicians that they co-operate with each other. The Chairman of a nationalized bank was asked to go on leave in 2004 for his refusal to extend a loan to three corporates to the tune of rupees 10 million each, as advised by an influential politician in the ruling party. Even after the change of guard, the new finance minister did not restore him his job, because he was considered a "useless non-performing banker". Those who figure as tainted officials in the website of the Central Vigilance Commission are often the most sought-after officials for being "most useful" to the corrupt politicians. The political interference in matters of appointment, promotion and transfer and charges of favouritism, nepotism and corruption have caused frustration to civil servants. The 2G scam, in which the Telecom secretary and the minister had gone to jail, the coal scam and the consequent harassment of honest civil servants are examples where the honest civil servants have not been able to fulfil their role because of political pressure.

The role of the civil servant in any country changes with the philosophy of the government in power, coupled with the stated aims and objectives of the State as enshrined in the Constitution by the founding fathers of the nation. In India the Constitution enacted and adopted by the constituent assembly on 26 January 1950 lays down the path on which the nation has to evolve, while the government in power decides the strategies to achieve the constitutional goals.

Why is civil service effective in India?

The effectiveness of the civil services in India is largely due to legacy inherited from the British rule in India coupled with the farsightedness of the post-independence political leaders. They realized that the outgoing colonial power had gifted the country a highly accomplished team of administrators committed to the nation. This human resource, which was used to control and subjugate India was redeployed for the all-round economic development and it's of the Indian democracy as an instrument of the state. The British had set up a strong system of administration in the basic unit called the District. The District Magistrate/ Collectors administered very large areas, some of them equivalent to independent countries of Europe. They were given immense powers of both revenue and police, and also administered justice under the Indian Penal Code.

The people living in the districts look up on the District Magistrate as a Semi-God.

In the absence of any political control over the civil servant right up to the time when legislative councils were introduced in the early years of the twentieth century, the civil servants were accountable only to the Governor/ Viceroy. They were asked with controlling the administering the district, ensuring peace and stability of British rule. This made the role of the civil servant very crucial.

Under the Government of India act 1935 and subsequently under the new Constitution of India adopted on January 26 1950, the Allocation of Business Rules promulgated by the President of India, it was clearly stated that the Secretary of the Department is the Administrative and Financial head of the department. True, he will work under the Minister in-charge of the Department/ Ministry, but no financial and administrative orders can be issued by a Minister. An order of the Ministry is legally and administrative leave valid only when it is issued under the signature of the Secretary of the Department.

Furthermore, under the All India Services Act, all the important and senior posts, both under the Central and State governments, are cadre posts only to be filled up by officer of the All India Services namely the IAS, the IPS and the Indian Forest Service. These All India Service Officers are recruited through the Union Public Service Commission on merit and appointed by the President of India under his seal. Thus, the Central Government ensures complete control over the working of the States through the civil servants.

The senior-most Indian Administrative Service Officers are selected for important post like that of Defence Secretary, Home Secretary, and Finance Secretary and so on in other departments. Amongst them, normally the senior most Secretary working in the Centre, is appointed as the Cabinet Secretary to the Government. He sits in all Cabinet meetings and processes the proposals of the various departments of the Government of India, before they are discussed in the Cabinet, where only Cabinet Ministers sit. The Cabinet Secretary can also return the proposals of the department if they do not conform to the Rules of Business as promulgated by the President of India. He is the most powerful officer in the Government of India and is the eyes and ears of the Prime Minister.

The Cabinet Secretary also has a committee called the Committee of Secretaries. Whenever there are differences between two or more departments, the Prime Minister directs the Committee of Secretaries to sort out the issue. The Cabinet Secretary then sits down with the departmental Secretaries and after discussions gives his verdict which is then accepted by the Prime Minister.

The Cabinet Secretary also examines proposals for appointment of officers to the posts of Joint Secretary, Additional Secretaries and Special Secretaries. These are then sent to the Appointments Committee of the Cabinet (ACC) for approval of the Prime Minister and Home Minister.

The Cabinet Secretary is given the same status and rank as the three Chiefs of Army, Navy and the Air Force. He is the primus inter pares amongst them. All the three Service Chiefs have to attend the meeting called by the Cabinet Secretary, whenever required.

The other civil servant who would be as powerful would be the Secretary to the Prime Minster, who scrutinizes all the files which came for approval of the Prime Minister. The Secretary to the Prime Minister is often the conduit through which the Prime Minister conveys his messages to the other Ministers.

A new but powerful post that has been created in the last two decades is the post of National Security Advisor. He advises the Prime Minister on Security issues. There is also a National Security Council headed by the NSA/ Deputy NSA, which analysis security issues and puts it up for perusal of the Prime Minister and the Cabinet Committee on Security (the CCS). These are all men by civil servants either from the IAS, or the Indian Police service or the Indian Foreign Service.

The government also has a vigilance organization called the Vigilance Commission. This is also headed by a civilian known as the Chief Vigilance Commissioner. The other members of the Commission are also civilian. The Vigilance Commission oversees the internal vigilance organizations of the various department and also conducts vigilance enquiries against public servants suspected of corruption. The Central Bureau of Investigation (the CBI) works under the guidance and supervision of the Vigilance Commission. This is indeed a very powerful organization of the Government.

The Comptroller and Auditor General

The chief auditor of the Government accounts is known as the Comptroller and Auditor General of India. He audits all the accounts of the Central and State Government Departments and points out the irregularities committed by these departments. His report is submitted to the President of India, who then directs the Government to place it on the Table of the House. Often governments have fallen because of the adverse report of the CAG. Once the report is placed on the Table of the House it is sent to the Public Accounts Committee (the PAC) for a detailed examination and recommendations. The Public Accounts Committee is mostly chaired by a seasoned political leader from the opposition benches.

All departmental Secretaries are called before the PAC to give their explanation on the adverse remarks made in the report. The CAG sits on the right hand of the Chairman of the PAC and advises him on the questions to be asked. The CAG all over the world is a very powerful post as the entire working of the government is on scrutiny. In India this post is also manned by retired officers of the civil service.

Indian foreign service

India has a highly professional Foreign Service called the Indian Foreign Service. It is manned by civilians, recruited by the Union Public Service Commission along with the All India and other Central services. After training they are posted either in the External Affairs Ministry or diplomatic Missions abroad. Since they don't move to other departments of the Government of India, they turn out to be extremely professional in their approach. It is very rare to have outsiders or politicians to head these diplomatic assignments. The Indian Foreign Service officers can compete with the best in the world. The Prime Minister usually has one a Foreign Service officer in his personal staff.

Representativeness and reservations in the civil services in India

The Indian civil service system reflects the characteristics of representativeness of Indian society in multifarious ways. There is no bar to persons belonging to different regions, caste and creeds, gender and religion joining the civil service. There is no bias for people with a particular educational background which could facilitate their entry to the civil Service. However, those who entered the Indian civil Service, one has to have a minimum age of 21 years (for the Indian Police Service it is 20 years). The maximum age is 28 years (except for the scheduled caste, tribes and backward classes). There are also reservations for handicapped people, apart from reservation for the Scheduled Castes/ Scheduled Tribes and other backward classes. Altogether 50% of the total seats for recruitment to the All India and Central services are reserved for the section of society as for the provision of the Constitution, as they were deprived of the benefit of development for several centuries.

The provincial or State cadre for the civil services are determined on the basis of the population of each State. For instance, Uttar Pradesh which is the biggest province in terms of population, has a strength of more than eight lakh civil servants excluding the teachers which numbers other six lakhs. Moreover, the strength of IAS officers in UP is another 560, whereas, the least populated state of Sikkim has below 50 IAS officers.

The central and All India Services are attracting candidates who have completed their Medical graduation as well as Engineers and IT professionals. It is because of the stature of All India Service officers enjoy the command they respect, since the British colonial rule. Since independence, the quality and merit of officers, including those appointed under the reserved quotas, and their selection have retained this legacy. It is the main reason why there is such a tough competition to enter the services. There is also a reservation of 30% for the State Civil Service officers in the State cadre of the IAS. It gives an opportunity to the State Civil Service officers to occupy important posts like that of District Magistrates and

Secretaries to the Government of the State. Sometimes, they also get postings in the Union Government.

A Civil servant normally retires at the age of 60 years after putting in more than 35 to 37 years of service, and thus enjoys a great deal of stability. They have nothing to do with the political structure as selections are not on regime type of party system but through the constitutionally provided Public Service Commission both at the Central and State level.

Politicisation

The post-independence civil service system has turned out to be different from what it used to be in British India where an Indian Civil Service officer used to be a member of the Council of Administrators. The members of the Council could be equivalent to a Minister administering the Indian subcontinent comprising the present-day India, Pakistan and Bangladesh. The Governor General use to head the Council. The Indian Civil Service officer, besides acting as a Minister, also head to take responsibility for implementing policy. In post independent India, under a newly elected Government, this privilege has been taken away. The scope of the functioning of the civil service has been limited only to implementation of the policy as conveyed by the Minister, unless of course the Minister asked for his advice. Thus, the civil servants, at both the Central and State levels, are charged with the responsibility of faithful execution of the government's policy on the promises made by the ruling party at the time of the polls.

The Civil servants make the political manifesto into an administrative document for its effective implementation. They have to pledge their sincerity not to a particular political party but to the political regime in power at any point of time.

The Minister became politically responsible for his department. If an issue was brought before the State legislature or Parliament, it was the Minister who answered the queries on the basis of the reply drafted by his Ministry/ Secretary. The British system and conventions became the models for the working of the Government, both at the Centre and State.

In this context, it is relevant to remember what Dr B.R. Ambedkar, Chairman of the drafting committee had stated in the constituent assembly and which philosophy primates the entire system in India.

"Whenever democratic institutions exists, experience has shown that it is essential to protect the civil service as far as possible from political or personal influence and to give in that position of stability and security which is vital to its successful working as an impartial and efficient instrument by which government of whatever complexion gives effect to their policies. It is imperative that our government which comes into power, the permanent time civil services must carry out the policies laid down by the government for the time being in office. In countries where this has been neglected, and where the spoils system has taken its place, inefficient and disorganised civil service has been the inevitable result and corruption has become rampant with all its attendant consequences".

He further goes on to say, "Otherwise I am afraid that the civil services will apprehend that amenability to Ministerial pressure and correct attitude towards questions in which a little cautery or the group for the time being in power, is interested, I will secure them promotions rather than merit or efficiency. I have often observed that a secretary to the Minister if he volunteers an opinion which is not palatable to the Ministers in office, the Minister puts him on the black list and he is not considered favourable for future promotions. Of course, once a policy is laid down, the public servants have to carry them out. But I know of instances where Ministers have looked upon with disfavour, Secretaries or other servants, whose opinion was seen as criticizing their policies; this is a very undesirable state of affairs and I am sure that sort of thing should not be encouraged. Therefore, I hold that where there is any apprehension on the part of civil servants that, if they are amenable to Ministerial pressure, they are likely to be promoted, and that merit or efficiency counts less, if that mentality seizes public servants, there is likely to be demoralization throughout the ranks of the service".

In India, the political and administration work together, to achieve socio-economic goals. Although, another member of the Constituent Assembly. Mr M. V. Kamath observed that the political ambition of the country could not be achieved without support of the Indian Civil Service, and hence continuation of the British legacy of the Indian civil service was necessary in independent India, it may be noted that in the initial years there was no love lost between the Civil servants and the politicians as their perceptions differed. However, harmony in working gradually evolved from sixties onwards. Though we still have complaints from the young IAS officers blaming the politicians for asking them to get involved in undesirable tasks, and to help them in unethical, illegal and social pursuits, the Civil servants have started to resist, whatever be the consequences.

Under the Civil Service conduct Rules, civil servants are not expected to participate in political activity, especially elections. In fact, one of the Prime Ministers of India, late Smt. Indira Gandhi, was removed from membership of Parliament, when her election was declared invalid as she had used the services of a public servant for her elections. Civil servants are also debarred from taking up post retirement job, for a period of two years immediately following their retirement, permission of the government is required for taking up assignments during this period, both in India and abroad. A very negligible number of civil servants have joined politics after their retirement. They have served well as Ministers too, because of their experience and understanding of the processes of governance.

From this it follows that the personnel policy in the civil service should be provided in the form of a balanced, coherent system of human impacts of different levels of social control: state, municipal, public and commercial.

Beyond the issues mentioned, the use of new technologies in the public sector introduces a number of philosophical discussions, such as the changing public perception of privacy, security and surveillance; or the ownership and exploitation of personal data, therefore, providing a rich domain for further interdisciplinary discussion.

New technologies provide powerful tools for future policy development and modelling. Public policy spans areas such as online monitoring of public opinion; community participation in policy development; and modelling proposed policies and statutes. Several tools and platforms have been developed to communicate with, integrate and empower citizens. The aim of these platforms is to encourage and facilitate partnerships between citizens and civic authorities, enabling individuals to play a greater role.

❑

CHAPTER 5

Role of the Civil Service in USA

The role of the Federal civil bureaucracy in USA is primarily to implement policies established by the Congressional Acts or Presidential decisions. The legislations, generally determine only the guidelines for meeting governmental goals, allowing bureaucrats to develop specific policies and programs. The bureaucracy includes a wide range of activities, from regulating the behaviour of individuals and corporations to buying everything from pencil to jet fighters for the government.

To exercise control over individuals and corporations, the civil servants make regulations. The regulations are made in a 'notice and comment procedure', in which proposed rules are published in the Federal Register and made available for debate by the general public. The process of devising or modifying regulations is extremely political as the bureaucrats need Congressional support to protect their budget.

The Street-level Bureaucracy

These are Agency employees who directly provide services to the public, such as those who provide job or skill training services. The Research and development are conducted by government scientists. The driving force of the development of bureaucracy has been a combination of new demands from citizens from enhanced government services and the desire of the people in government to respond to these demands or to increase the size and scope of the federal government in line with their own policy goals.

Until 1928, the American bureaucracy had no more than a few thousand members and there were only three executive departments (State, Treasury and War). The early federal government performed a narrow range of tasks, which reflected the then philosophy of governance. With the election of Andrew Jackson in 1928, came a spoils systems, in which people who had worked on his campaign, were rewarded with positions in government. Because these new employees often lacked experience, detailed procedures and routines were developed to guide their actions.

As America expanded, so did the size of the federal government. The federal government's role in daily life was still limited, though it employed significantly more people to support the increased geographic area.

The Progressive Era

Changes in the second half of the nineteenth century dramatically increased the government's regulatory powers. The federal civil service, created by the 1883 Pendleton Civil Service Act, ensured that bureaucrats would be hired on the basis of merit rather than political connections. Driving these changes was a shift in citizen's demands. People wanted a greater role for government, both in regulating the large corporations and delivering more services to the citizens.

The New Deal, the Great Society and the Reagan Revolution

The New Deal refers to the Governments' program implemented during Franklin Roosevelt's first term as President in the 1930's. These programs were a response to the Great Depression and aimed to stimulate employment, economic growth and the formation of labour unions. The size, responsibilities and capacity of the bureaucracy were expanded and enhanced. Many Republicans were opposed to this expansion. They were apprehensive that a much heavier Federal Government outfit might not be able to deliver services efficiently.

The Great Society was a further expansion in the size, capacity and activities of the bureaucracy that occurred during the Presidency of Lyndon Johnson (1963-69). The enhanced funding for education, transit, health-care and civil rights impacted the welfare of the socially disadvantageous sections. These social sector initiatives contributed to the dramatically increased political participation by African Americans. The election of Barack Hussain Obama as the 44th President for two terms (2009-2017) shows the social and political maturity of the USA. The unanimous approval of the appointment of the air force chief, General Charles Brown in June 2020 in the US Senate is yet another example of the evolution of a plural society. General Brown is the first African-American military service chief to be elevated to the coveted position. In the Senate the vote was 98-0. Its significance is because the appointment was ratified in the upper house amidst the country wide racial riots.

In the US, the efforts of the antipoverty measures could not deliver the expected results. There was a lack of understanding within the bureaucratic systems about the specific needs of the deprived sections. In India, the bureaucracy is trained at the district-level and is quite aware of the challenges of implementing a specific programme. Therefore, it is not surprising that many anti-poverty programs initiated during the Johnson period failed. Many of the people who designated and implemented these programmes did not understand the complexity of the problems they were trying to address.

The Reagan administration (1980-88) created an opportunity for conservatives to roll back the size and scope of the Federal Government. The growth of the federal government, however, did not show. Until the present day, few government programs have been eliminated, and the federal budget has steadily increased.

Evolution of Modern Federal Bureaucracy

The Executive Office of the President (EOP) contains organizations that support the President and implement Presidential policy initiatives. The Office of Management and Budget, for example, is considered for creating the President's Annual Budget proposal to Congress, reviewing proposed rules, and other budget related tasks. Below the EOP are the fifteen executive departments, as mentioned above. The head of these fifteen organizations make up the President's cabinet.

The Federal Government serves a wide range of functions. Furthermore, the division of activities, amongst executive departments and independent agencies does not have an obvious logic. It has been often noticed that in such organizations, elected officials make attempts to shape agency behaviour. In general, organizations that are housed within an executive department, can be controlled by the President to some extent through his appointees, but independent agencies have more freedom from oversight and control by the President and Congress.

With the growing needs of the people, the size of the Federal Government has expanded. It employs millions of people to serve the various fields. The citizens of US are becoming more and more demanding. The surveys and opinion polls reveal that there is little demand for less government. It could be attributed to the fact that in the contemporary world US has emerged as the most powerful nation in the world.

Civil Services Regulations

Federal salaries are supposed to be comparable to what people earn in similar private sector positions. Education determines the position for which a person is eligible to apply. A set of tests is used to determine who is hired for low level clerical and secretarial positions, while higher level jobs are filled by comparing the qualifications and experience of candidates who meet the educational qualifications for the position.

The civil service regulations provide job security. After three years of satisfactory performance, employees cannot be fired except “for cause”. It is possible, however, to reduce the size of the federal workforce through reductions in force (RIF) which are occasionally carried out when an entire office or program is terminated.

There are many regulations that exist regarding civil service to insulate services from the partisan politics and policy. It has made it difficult for elected officials to control the hiring and firing of government employees, and it also hinders them from furthering their own political goals with a partisan approach.

The Political Appointees and the Senior Executive Service

Not every Federal employee is a member of the civil service. The President appoints over 7000 individuals to senior positions in the executive branch that are not subject to civil service regulations. Some government agencies have the reputation of being "turkey farms", agencies where campaign workers and donors are often appointed to reward them for their service, because it is unlikely that their lack of qualifications will lead to bad policy.

The majority of the President's appointees are intended to act as the President's eyes, ears and hands throughout the executive branch. In many agencies, people, who serve in the top positions are members of the Senior Executive Service (SES). They are also exempt from civil service regulations. The President's nominees in the higher bureaucracy in different agencies enable him, to reorient the new administration for implementing his policies. The SES also gives civil servants an incentive to do their jobs well, because it may lead to their promotion in SES.

Senior Executive Service

The Senior Executive Service is a position classification in the civil federal service of USA, equivalent to general officer or Flag Officer ranks in the US Armed Forces. It was created in 1979.

Up to 10% of SES positions can be filled as political appointments rather than by career employees. About half of the SES is designated "Career reserved", which can be filled by career employees. The other half is designated "General" which can be filled by either career employees or political appointments as desired by the administration. Due to the 10% limitation, most General positions are still filled by career appointees.

Senior level employees of several agencies are exempt from the SES but have their own senior executive positions, these include the FBI, CIA, Defence Intelligence Agency, National Security Agency, Members of Foreign Service, the Government-owned corporations, etc.

Handling Crisis in the USA- Two World-Wars and Covid-19

Wars always produce a tilt towards the growth of Government. Wars leave in their wake "mass of officeholders". Further in each major war, the government became the preeminent player on the economic stage and when the war was over, the government never completely reverted to the status of a "bit player". Jonathon Hughes says, "Each war inflated the economy and gave the Federal spending mechanism a scope it did not previously have. The historical expansion of the Federal sector has been mainly achieved by a few short bursts of war-time spending, not by a steady rise relating to the country's population growth, or the GNP it produced. After each war there were expanded interest payments, new benefits for veterans, as well as the actual growth of government costs".

Military spending showed a sharp increase over the pre-war years. America found dangerous new rivals in the world scene, and could not return to its pre-war isolationism.

Certain agencies expanded more rapidly than the GNP. The Railway Retirement Board increased dramatically over the war years. The growth of the Treasury Department was because there was much increased debt to manage and heavier taxes to collect. The demand for the Treasury's services was derived from the demand for veterans' benefits, military strength etc. the demand after the First World War and later after the Second World War, to play a more decisive role in world affairs required a large volume of resources to create the framework through which American power could be asserted.

The income tax base was considerably broadened during the war. Many people were brought under the tax net, who had never paid taxes on their income before; the rates were increased, and payroll withholding was introduced. The country got used to large federal deficit and consequent tax on wealth too was introduced. The government could mop up high tax revenues without much resistance. It could be attributed to the higher inflation, which could elevate people into higher income brackets, thus the government could impose taxes to enhance its revenue without any overt resistance.

The federal employment saw a rise in the federal share of the Labour force during the war years. The increase in the World War-I period (1913-1922) was from 1.02% to 1.28%. During the World War-II period (1939-1945) the federal share in offering employment rose from 2.03% to 3.36%. The federal agencies engaged in war efforts recruit a large number of employees during war time. They insist that the new workers needed to perform essential or crucial aid to the ongoing war efforts. The Congress tends to go slow on layoffs after the war. It could be related to the possible political implications, if a large number of employees are sacked, thus the federal bureaucracy continued to expand. The demand for more services and expectations from the federal administration enhanced the number of employees. It was due to the obvious long-term costs of the wars. The bulk of the increase was noticed mostly in three units-the defence establishment, the Post Office and the Veterans' Administration. This is because during war, the public changes its attitudes towards defence, and is sympathetic towards rewarding Veterans' for their wartime services.

The wartime technological innovations, military training of pilots, and the transfer of capital created for war purposes to the private sector- all of these favoured the development of commercial aviation. This expanded the role of the Aeronautical Authority as well as the Weather Bureau. This again promoted increased Federal employment. The Atomic Energy Commission also became a major employer by 1949.

During the War, a number of agencies were also set up by the President or the Congress. By a rough count there were 131 new agencies set up during the war period. They served to dramatize the government's response to a particular problem. New agencies also permitted new approaches to problems that might have been barred by the long run commitments of certain existing agencies.

The Executive Office of the President also saw a massive expansion. The spending in this administrative division increased from 11.1 billion to 1941 to a peak of

408.1 billion in 1945. All of this was accounted for by spending by emergency agencies housed in this division. These included the War Production Board, the Foreign Economic Administration, the Office of War information, the Office of Defense transportation and War Manpower Commission among many others.

The First World War witnessed a vast mobilization nearly five million men in all and again an almost complete demobilization after the war. The Second World War involved 1.6 million military personnel. The demobilization that followed was less complete than after previous engagements owing to the development of the Cold War, but it was substantial nevertheless. The Army fell in size from over eight million men to only half a million.

A study of the effect of World War-II on USA economy shows that war immediately triggered off the new opportunities: eligible men went to war, and women went to work at factories or in other jobs to replace the men. Factories operated round the clock to produce the armaments, material, and clothes necessary to equip, shelter and dress a huge army

During World War-II the Federal Government, as we saw above continued to grow and expand tremendously to meet the needs of a nation at war. During World War-I, the bureaucracy was reorganized on the basis of the wartime Overman Act of 1918, which authorized the President "to consolidate bureaus, agencies and offices—in the interest of the economy and the more efficient operation of the government".

After the United States became involved in the World War-II, the President was again given extensive authority under the War Powers Act of 1941 to restructure federal military and civilian bureaus. The legislation provided however, that all government functions altered by the President during the War were to return to their pre-war status when the conflict ended.

The war sparked off the creation of new kind of jobs and massive public and private spending that finally lifted the United States out of its pristine agriculture-based economic systems into a vibrant economy with a large industrial base. It was a mammoth effort in which the vast majority of America's industrial and human resources were brought to bear. Huge naval ships were built in weeks; then in days. America made all vehicles but the Russian Army was on wheels.

Sacrifice was the mantra of the day. The nation's two major labour union federations, the AFL and the CIO, agreed not to strike. Americans, sometimes grudgingly, submitted to the Federal government's rationing of everything from gasoline, to shoes and food. New automobiles, radios and other big-ticket items were virtually unavailable for purchase. In addition to rationing, the government coordinated the use of raw materials and the production of staple goods. Indeed during the war, the federal government played even a larger role in the functioning of the American economy than it did during the New Deal. In the process, the Roosevelt administration ran up massive deficits.

There is no gainsaying the fact that World War-II, brought further administrative growth. Federal management of the wartime economy stabilized material life for unprecedented numbers of Americans. Wartime production boosted domestic employment, while militia service provided other economic possibilities. None of this would have been possible without the civil servants to ensure programs ran smoothly.

USA and the Covid-19 Crisis

The United States, which has the most expensive health care infrastructure in the world, remained by far the country most adversely affected by the coronavirus pandemic with more than 3.5 million cases and around 1,40,000 fatalities as on July 15th 2020. These problematic conditions were created by a seriously flawed response to Covid-19 from its initial identification till date.

The biggest failure in the US was perhaps the saga of botched SARS-Cov-2 testing kits sent out by the Center for Disease Control and Prevention (CDC) in early February. The kits did not work correctly and because the Food and Drug Administration (FDA) didn't allow outside labs to create their own tests until the end of February. This delayed action allowed unrestricted spread of COVID-19 for weeks. It exposed the inability of the decision makers that due to the delayed decision precious weeks were lost.

There were little COVID-19 testing facilities in the United States and so little sense of the scope of the looming crisis. For this failure of the Government, both the public health bureaucracy and the medical device bureaucracy should share the blame.

The decisions were made on the basis of political considerations rather than adopting scientific approach and enlisting the support of each component of the administration to save the people. Initially, the Government was dismissive of the menace of the Corona Virus comparing it to the seasonal flu! The Vice President, Mike Pence, was appointed to head a task force to advice on what to do to tackle this grave crisis, but he was not given any real authority. The US Pandemic Response Team, which was formed to combat public health crisis had been disbanded. If it was realized that pandemic is nothing but a sort of a biological war, the issue to reduce the federal bureaucracy should not have been raised at all. The Corona Virus crisis revealed that outcome of the long campaign to reduce the bureaucracy. The administrative state was left ill equipped to protect the nation's citizens, leaving state and local governments to pick up the pieces. Governors and mayors scrambled to get adequate medical equipment as the doctors sounded alarm over the shortages. Federal government refused to help. The same attitude influenced decisions about closing schools and businesses and attempts to ramp up virus testing capacity. The Federal Government refused to take up the leadership to combat this crisis. In India, on the other hand it was the Central

Government that took the lead and guided the states in combating the crisis.

In USA, unlike India, the pandemic was treated as a state and local issue. There was no standardized federal intervention on the pandemic. The Governors and local officials were made responsible for handling it. As a result, the approaches and results varied considerably from state to state.

No national plan, backed by law was devised to address the pandemic. India had its Disaster Management Act and the Epidemic Act under which the Central Government could statutorily enforce its decisions, but no such law existed in USA. The Vice President's Task Force developed guidelines for States and localities for testing, tracking and treatment of the Virus; sheltering in place; and, the use of masks and social distancing to prevent its spread. However, these remained only as guidelines, not mandatory rules or law, as it is in India.

In USA, another shortcoming was the limited national access to testing, medical equipment and supplies. The federal government furnished a nominal amount of these, but the supplies and supply chain were woefully insufficient. The states were left on their own to source the life-saving equipment etc., and fought among themselves, to acquire these materials from overseas and private sources. In India, on the other hand, when the Center found that the Government of Delhi was short of ventilators and personal protection equipment kits, it was the Centre which rushed in supplies and helped the beleaguered state. It may be noted that the two governments belong to different political parties, but the resources were pooled to serve each region or state.

In USA also unlike India, there was a push towards rapid reopening. The Federal Government was always opposed to sheltering and staying at home. The US President himself tweeted to his millions of party men to liberate States such as Virginia and Michigan, where he felt the Governors were going quite slowly in reopening.

The policy of reopening one part, based on the relative success in another, ignored the nature of the disease. The original hotspots for the pandemic were primarily States and urban cities in the Northeast and the Midwest and California. During the mid-May to early weeks of June, the spread was weakening in these locations and appeared to have peaked around the country. The states such as Georgia, Florida, Texas and Arizona faced the ferocity of the epidemic. They became the new hot spots, ahead with relative rapid reopening. Unlike India, the USA could not evolve a centralized monitoring mechanism to watch the spread of the virus and could take prompt actions to control the deadly virus. In spite of having large medical facilities, USA became the country with the highest number of infections and deaths due to epidemic across the world.

It is unfortunate that the US establishment comprising its legislature and political executives, both at the federal, state and local bodies could not measure up to this biological war. It is hardly surprising that they were more concerned towards their respective authorities within the constitution then to work and evolved uniform enforcement mechanism. In India, the civil administration, the police the state and Central authorities acted in unison and every step or directions issued were in consultation with the health authorities at the states as well as union levels.

On the other hand, the response to the pandemic was delayed and the state did not observe focused approach in enforcing current time at the respective persons home itself the wearing of mass and social distancing where it in each state causing spread of the varies. In some States such as Georgia and Texas with Republican governors and large cities with democratic measures were the government only recommended these actions to build Covid-19, while the mayor's required them by the law.

Frank F Islam, in his analysis of the crisis, has pointed that in USA there was a misplaced prioritization of economic concerns over health concerns. A balance between the two should have been maintained as in India. The re-openings in USA were done almost solely to stimulate the economy which had suffered due to the pandemic. For this lack of focus, the American had to suffer unprecedented fatalities. He has further pointed out that in USA there was the consistent rejection and discounting of expert advice. The advice of experts was not given due importance, especially by the political decision makers at the apex. The suggestions given by the internationally renowned expert Dr. Anthony Fauci were ignored, and the pandemic went out of control. In India the Indian Council of Medical Research was the prime mover in all decisions of the Union Government and the state administration, and that is why India performed much better in the Covid-19 crisis despite having meagre resources in comparison to USA. In India, the health experts, scientists, political executive and bureaucracy functioned in unison and acted proactively, while the US Federal and State Governments acted reactively. This made all the difference.

Relationship between the Federal Government and the States

Article IV of the US Constitution establishes the responsibilities of the State to each other and the responsibilities of the Federal Government towards the States. Section 1 of Article IV requires that the State give "full faith and credit" to the public acts and judicial proceedings of every other state. In other words, it states that the states must honour each other's decisions and legal judgements; section 2 stipulates that the citizens of each state are entitled to all privileges and immunities of citizens in other states. For example, the Supreme Court ruled that as California law denying new residents welfare benefits for a year was unconstitutional.

One reason for the ongoing negotiations over the balance between state and the federal government is there exclusive and concurrent power. Exclusive powers are those powers reserved to the federal Government of the state. Concurrent power is power shared by the federal Government and the states.

Exclusive Federal Powers	Concurrent Powers	Exclusive State Powers
Coining Money	Taxation	Conducting elections
Regulating interstate and establishing local	Law making and enforcement	Foreign commerce governments
Regulating the mail providing Public Safety	Chartering Bank and Corporations health, welfare	Declaring war, maintaining militia Taking land for public use
Raising armies ratifying constitution	Establishing courts	Amendments
Conducting foreign affairs	Borrowing money, Regulating intra-sate	Commerce
Establishing inferior courts	Establishing rules of naturalization	

The exclusive powers of the federal government help the nation operate as a unified whole.

The States retain a lot of power, however

States conduct elections even presidential elections and must ratify constitutional amendments. So long as their laws do not contradict national laws, state governments can prescribe policies on commerce, taxation, healthcare, education and many other issues within their state.

Notably, both the states and the federal Government have the power to tax, make and enforce laws, charter banks and borrow money.

Changing Distribution of Power

The changing distribution of power between states and the federal government, the balance of power between states and the federal government has changed a great deal over time. In the early United States, the division between state powers and federal power was very clear. The state regulated within their borders, and the federal government regulated National and international issues. However, since the civil war in 1860's, the Federal Government's powers have overlapped and intertwined with state powers. In times of crisis like the great depression of the nineteen thirties, the federal government had has stepped in to provide much needed financial assistance in the sectors, typically under the jurisdiction of the state.

Although the general trend has been towards an increase in federal power, the states have also pushed back, for example, in the 1995 case US vs Lopez, the Supreme Court ruled that the federal government had overstepped it's bounds, by claiming the authority to ban guns from school grounds under the Commerce clause. Because guns on school grounds are not related to interstate commerce, the Supreme Court ruled that gun ban unconstitutional.

One way that the federal government can influence the states is through the distribution of grants and incentives, and aid. The State and local government are eager to obtain federal assistance, but most of these financial helps is accompanied by strings attached to the use of grants. The civil servants deployed at the federal level use the power of money to persuade state and local bodies to tow the federal line. The categorical grants from the federal government can only be used for specific purposes and frequently include provinces non-discrimination provisions (saying that the distribution of the funds cannot be for purposes that discriminate against women, minorities or other groups.

The Federal government can also pass unfunded mandates that tie federal funding to certain conditions. For example, the National Minimum Drinking Act of 1984 stipulated that States must have a minimum drinking age of 21 in order to receive full federal highway funding. Not all federal funding is strictly monitored. Block grants are federal grants given to states or localities for broad purposes. The state or local governments can then disburse funds as they see fit.

Unlike India, civil servants of the Federal government do not work or get transferred to the state government. They, therefore, are not aware of the problems of the state governments. In India, a civil servant earns a job by qualifying in a fierce highly competitive examination. The young officers work at the district level and when they are inducted in the service of the Union, they have a vast experience of serving the countryside. In USA, there is no experience of the officials serving in the Federal structure of the State administration. The Federal governments has little role either in the selection of the State civil services or regulating their service conditions.

However, when, in the 1930's, the NEW DEAL brought new federation registration for implementing several programs and policies geared towards reviving the economic, the seeds of cooperative federalism began taking roots requiring the federal civil servants to work closely with the state civil servants? It led to the concept of cooperative federalism. It took strong roots by the year 1945.

The cooperative federalism become necessary due to growing responsibilities of the Federal State. In many areas, their functioning and their responsibilities were intertwined. The federal and state governments corporate, or work together, to provide services. For example, state governments often administer federal programs and states often depend on federal grants to support state government programs.

State governments eventually become dependent on the federal government in order to administer many of their programs, like housing and transportation. This led to a subject of cooperative federalism known as creative federalism. Creative federalism favours the federal government by creating a dependency on the federal government. This strengthens the federal civil service. Because the state depended on federal financial grants, creative federalism weakened state powers and strengthened federal powers. This type of federalism was used by the federal civil servants and was used through the year of 1960's.

New Federalism

In the 1970's, the US moved towards New Federalism. New Federalism allows the states to reclaim some power while recognizing the federal government as the highest governmental power. It was a response to the argument that the federal government grew too powerful and overshadowed many of the responsibilities originally reserved to the States.

New Federalism is based on the political philosophy of devolution. Devolution is the transfer of certain power from the federal government to the states. President Nixon was the first US President to openly support new federalism. Nixon served as President from 1969 to 1974, as new federalism first took root. However new federalism is mostly associated from President Ronald Reagans years from 1981 to 1989.

Reagan thought federal grants were improperly used to impose the interests of the federal government on the individual states. With the new federalism, the federal government provides large block grants, or block of money, to the states to be used for social programs. Unlike in previous years, the states have broad discretion to implement the programs they best see fit. The federal government mostly only monitors the progress and outcomes of these projects. This obviously strengthens the hold of the federal bureaucracy over the states' bureaucracy.

State and Local Government Employment

Over the last 25 years, the story of state and local employment has been one of growth in scale and scope alike. While variations exist in state by state comparisons and across local jurisdictions, govt. employment at the state level grew by 35% overall. Nationally, state and local governments employed about 7.4 million full time equivalent workers in 2014 (Latest statistics not available) That's approximately 232 public employees for every 10,000 Americans, according to Governing calculations of Census survey data. Including teachers and those working in education the total doubles to about 16.2 million 1public employees (excluding federal government) nationwide.

Across states, government employment statistics vary greatly. Unique circumstances tend to account for high or very low concentrations of public employment.

Wyoming, for example, employs the most public employees per capita largely due to the public hospitals that it operates. It is followed by Alaska, which has far more natural resources and highways workers than other states.

The broad distribution of state and local employment category wise is given below (in 2004)

Elementary/ Secondary Education

Financial administration	394,657
Corrections	701,112
Fire Protection	345,988
Health	434,696
Higher Education	2,077,077
Highways	491,042
Hospitals	978,816
Judicial and Legal	407,597
Natural Resources	171,239
Police Protection	905, 254
Public Welfare	506013

There were 21,995,000 employed by federal, state and local governments in the USA last year. All governments currently employ about 2.88 million full time employees as in January 2020. States with the most federal civilian employees were California, the District of Columbia, Virginia, Maryland and Texas. The US Federal government is the biggest employer in the United States even taking into account the private sector corporations etc.

Civil Servants and Politics

The Hatch Act of July 1940 makes it illegal for anyone receiving his pay, even in part, from federal funds to be politically active. This means state and local employees who work on cooperative programs such as highways and agricultural aid, paid in whole or on part from federal money, cannot engage in politics. Cases involving just such employees come before the Civil Service Commission from time to time.

The United State Civil Service Commission enforces this provision of the Hatch Act. It has been possible only in the last four or five years to say truthfully that the great body of federal employees are really neutral politically and protected from partisan influence. The exception of course, is the policy determining positions.

Marlowe, in his 2004 study, sought to come closer to understanding public administrator's contribution to the improvement of the trust in government. He found that citizens either trusted the whole system or they did not trust any part of it, the civil service included. Central to good governance are sound attitudes towards the political and administrative institutions of a given society. Trust in these institutions has been among the leading issues on scholarly agendas in political science and public administration for many decades. It is one of the most important foundations upon which rests the legitimacy and sustainability of a political system. The theory of democracy is based on the most basic premise that citizens of a given polity entrust their sovereignty to a set of institutions that will decide for them and in their best interest.

While we address the determinants of trust in the civil service, the purpose is not the estimation of these predictors per se. Instead, we are most interested about the criteria citizens use to evaluate the level of trust in the civil service.

If citizen trust can be found to be a prerequisite for good governance, it is a policymaker′s duty to ask what may promote better levels of trust. There are many theoretical and empirical explanations of what should predict trust in government, but in the case of public administration, there is still much potential for comparative public opinion research from an interdisciplinary perspective.

While various attempts to implement systems for innovation have been made in the past, the results of these efforts have not been significant as they focused on partial institutional reorganisation, and they were also based on short-term prescriptions. There has been no effort to develop and manage human capital on a mid to a long-term perspective, which would enable us to predict and respond to future environmental changes on a pre-emptive basis. Consequently, there exists a significant gap between predicted environmental changes and the present reality. Thus, there exists a persistent need to encourage continuous and persistent innovation throughout the public sector personnel system.

According to the traditional compliance model, trust leads to legitimacy in the eyes of the public, which, in turn, leads to public cooperation with authoritative institutions. Compliance theories are built on the argument that test processes, as opposed outcomes, in developing trust and, hence, legitimacy and cooperation with institutions. Testing compliance theories, through latent variable factor analyses and structural equation modelling, would not only allow us to see to what extent process-based factors as opposed to outcome-based factors are relevant in determining trust, but it would allow us to consolidate evidence once on which institutions citizens would comply with the most, hence demonstrating that they differentiate among institutions.

❑

CHAPTER 6

Role of Civil Services in China

In the early 1950s, all administrators, managers and professionals (cadres) were managed centrally by the Chinese Communist Party's organisation department. The cadres, who worked in government agencies, bur known as 'government work personnel' or administrative work personnel. In 1950, the Ministry of Personnel was re-established. Because the CCP inherited government agency staff by Nationalist Party bureaucrats, who in the wake of the civil war were undoubtedly perceived to be unreliable, CCP cells were installed in all government agencies, headed by an appointed party Secretary: party committees were also established in all government offices to supervise the 'party life' activities of party members; and the vetting of all appointments and dismissal of leading civil servants, down to the rank of section chief, was turned over to the CCP through its " nomenklatura" system.

The Government agencies were staffed from several sources: university students assigned to some government jobs upon graduation: demobilized soldiers from the People's Liberation Army; and cadres from factories and units such as hospitals and schools. Only in the 1980s, after the reforms to prepare place for the centrally planned economy were underway, were these methods supplemented by efforts to recruit middle school graduates through advertising and competitive examinations.

The CCP established selection criteria that emphasized both talent and virtue. With the 1949 Revolution, the party loyalty continued to be an important criterion for the selections. The country's radical red guards occupied government offices and rounded up most incumbent cadres for periods of forced labour in the countryside. All State personnel agencies were abolished and the People's Liberation Army took over direct control of personnel work, including management of the Civil Service. In 1993, a separate management system for car dealers who work in government agencies was established and these cadres become 'civil servants.'

China's new civil service system included some innovations: entry to open competitive examinations; compensation level based on market rates; and a civil service managed by law. The selection of civil servants continued to be based on talent and virtue, which continued to be defined, in part, in terms of party loyalty. Although, officially, management of the civil service was vested in the Ministry of Personnel, it continued to work under the leadership of the party's Organisation Department (Burns). A senior CCP Politburo member continued to manage 'organisation and personnel work.'

China's post 1949 Constitutions have stipulated that the executive is 'responsible to the legislature' (called people's congresses). The State functionaries are urged in the Constitution to rely on the support of the people, keep in close touch with them, heed their opinion and suggestions, accept their supervision and do their best to serve them (article 27). The same language is repeated in 1993 Provisional Regulations (article 6) which also calls on Civil servant to 'work selflessly in the public interest.'

China's changing political and environment have had a major impact on the civil service system. The revolutions of 1911 and 1949 prompted constitutional change that changes the operational rules of the system (Burns). In 1992 when the CCP officially endorsed a 'socialist market economy with Chinese characteristics' as the future policy forced additional operational changes.

China has adopted a rigid and relatively narrowly defined position classification that places all civil servants in one of 12 positions ranged on 15 grades. The positions are divided into leadership and non- leadership positions. Because 98% of civil servants are employed locally, a major impediment to advancement is structural. Thus, civil servants employed by towns and townships, the lowest administrative grade, are confined to the three lowest positions (grades 9 to 15, while civil servants employed by counties) the next highest administrative grade, are confined to positions from grade 8 to 15.

The official criteria for becoming a Civil servant, includes "support to the leadership of the CCP and support of socialism. All candidates have to be screened for political correctness. Another odd feature is that for post in the Central Government, only Beijing residents are eligible.

In China, a single political/administrative elite rules the country. The Provisional Regulations lay down that the civil service system shall uphold the four basic principles (article 2) one of which is to uphold the leadership of the CCP. Civil service promotions are still controlled by the CCP through the nomenklatura system. All promotions to leadership positions have to be vetted by the relevant party cell or party committee organisation.

During periods of political crisis and leadership division, such as the Anti Rightist Campaign (1957), The Great Leap Forward (1958) and The Cultural Revolution (1966-76), and in the immediate aftermath of episodes such as the demonstrations in 1986 and 1989, political loyalty has been stressed as the paramount selection criteria for civil servants (Harding). Civil servants can mainly vote in elections and stand for office; further according to the Constitution, they have the right of free speech, press, assembly, association, procession and demonstration. However, they cannot participate in anti-government activities, including processions, demonstrations and strikes (Article 31).

The Government has also adopted affirmative action programs that have specially facilitated the employment of national minority officials in National minority areas. According to the Regulations, local governments are required to give preference to National minority applicants for civil jobs.

❑

CHAPTER 7

The State, Local and Country Bureaucracy in India, USA and China

State and Local Administration in India

The pattern of administration laid down by the British, both at state and local levels, was followed in independent India. The constitution, adopted by India on 26 January 1950, clearly laid down the functions of the Union and State governments under the seventh schedule. The functions of both were clearly demarcated under the heading of the Union list, state list and concurrent list. The delineation of subjects on which the central government or the state could legislate is an essential part of the federal structure. The concurrent list includes subject in which both the centre and States can legislate. Any law enacted by parliament in the concurrent list can be superseded by the legislation enacted by any state, only after Presidential approval.

Each state has its administrative apparatus similar to the structure in the union government. Each department is headed by a Secretary, with a full complement of additional secretaries, joint secretaries, and deputy secretaries, under-secretaries, section officers and assistants. During the colonial era, the bureaucracy was not top heavy. It expanded due to the greater role of the state in the field of economic development, health care and education.

The Secretary is the administrative, as well as that financial head of the department. The mandate of each department is laid down in the allocation of business rules as well as the rules of business promulgated by the President of India. The vast bureaucracy in the union government is supervised by the cabinet secretary, who is also the head of the civil services for the entire country. In the states, the corresponding position is that of the chief secretary and all the heads of the ministries are under his administrative control. In each department the senior officer gives an annual confidential remark (ACR) to his junior officers. The officer's promotion as well as his posting depend on these ACR's .

In the union government, the postings of officers at the level of joint secretary and above are approved by the appointments committee of the cabinet, on the recommendations of the cabinet secretary. In the states, the senior level postings are discussed between the chief secretary, the appointment secretary and the chief minister and appointment orders are issued thereafter. In the Rules of business, it is clearly laid down, that Government orders are those issued by any government official, who may be an Under-secretary, Deputy secretary, Joint secretary, etc. If the minister has to issue any official order, he has to get those orders issued under signatures of any of the officers of the Ministry. He cannot issue any government order under his signature, directly. So in India, the bureaucracy, selected on the basis of merit, plays a key role in implementing the political commitments made during the polls. Many bureaucrats are also inducted in the higher position of the political setup. There are instances of appointing Finance minister and also Foreign ministers, drawn from the bureaucracy.

One more interesting aspect in India is, that the senior most cadre posts can only be manned by the officers of the Indian Administrative Service officers, except in some few cases where they can be filled by officers of the central services or other All India Service officers

By manning the top post in the states, the constitution ensures the unity of the country. All these officers belonging to the IAS, IPS, Forest Service, and other Central government services are appointed under the signature and seal of the President of India. The governors in the state are the appointing authorities of the state civil service officers.

In the central government, officers are appointed on the recommendation of the Union Public Service Commission, while in the states, the state Civil servants are appointed on the recommendation of the State Public Service Commissions.

Below the state level we have districts headed by civil servants, who are designated as District Magistrates and Collectors. From the British period the district became the basic unit of governance. The District Magistrate is responsible for the law and order of the district, as well as revenue collection for the government, in addition to promoting development schemes, initiated by the Government from time to time. In India, the system has stood the test of time.

In USA, the police used massive violence to curb the rioters in the recent racial riots. On the other hand, the democratic values deeply inculcated in the Indian political system, help the bureaucracy to interact with the dissenters with minimum use of police.

On the other hand, the partitioned part of India, comprising Pakistan's two wings, the west and the east, despite the massive support of the western powers, could not keep the country united. Pakistan's predominant Sunni Muslim army committed genocide on its own citizens, killing 3 million men and women and violating and raping about a million women, though they belonged to the same Sunni sect. Unfortunately, the world's most powerful democracy, USA and its President, Richard Nixon, and his security advisor Henry Kissinger supported the genocide in 1971. It was India, her army, and her bureaucracy with the support of the political leadership of the Bengali Muslims, which helped in making Bangladesh independent. The people's rights and functioning of democracy in the country could be preserved successfully in a large measure due to the devoted and highly efficient civil services of Bangladesh.

In USA, it is heartening, that the political leadership, irrespective of their political ideology, appears to be slowly following the concept of the plural society enshrined in the Indian Constitution. The US Senate's unanimous endorsement of General Charles Q Brown, an African American, as the next Air force chief of staff, is quite heartening.

The Democratic Party's vice president nominee, Kamala Harris, who represents the confluence of two races, Black and Indian, also reveals that the US society appears to have graduated from the era of slavery of blacks, to accepting a merit-based system. Brown's elevation, amidst racial violence, shows the maturity of the America's political establishment in the recent years.

The Indian experience of making the district administration as a pivotal agency for all development work, including timely inputs to the farmers, like seeds and fertilizers appeared over the years to be highly paternal and centralised. This role is quietly being shifted to local bodies following the amendment in the Indian Constitution.

The collector or the district magistrate supervises all the district heads of the various government departments. He is the government representative on the field and he wields immense power both under the law or otherwise. The institutional role of the collector is quite interesting. As a part of the administration, the collector's role is of an employee of the government, but the role changes during the elections. The collector then functions as the instrument of the state ensuring non- partisan, fair and free elections. During the polls, the collector is responsible for their peaceful conduct. He is the Returning officer for the elections of the Members of Parliament. In this system, the supremacy of the civil authority is also ensured. The police chief or the district superintendent of police works in close coordination with the collector to ensure and maintain law and order in the district.

The post of a collector is a cadre post of Indian Administrative Service (IAS) and only IAS officers can man these posts. State civil service officers called the PCS (Provincial Civil Service) officers can only man post below the rank of District Magistrate. However in the IAS service rules, there is a provision through which 33% of the IAS posts in the states are to be filled by promotion from the PCS.

Whereas an IAS officer, theoretically, can be posted in any part of India, as it is an All India Service, but normally they continue to work in the IAS cadre of the state they are allotted to.

Apart from the IAS and IPS as well as the PCS, there are numerous other state services like

1. Block Development/Additional Block Development Officers Service

2. State agriculture service
3. Assistant forest Conservator/ forest range officer
4. Assistant registrar
5. UP judicial service
6. Assistant prosecuting officers
7. Nagar Palika (centralised) health Services: food and sanitary inspectors
8. Tehsildar /naib tehsildar
9. Panchayati Raj officers
10. Finance and accounts service
11. State VAT (value added tax)/sales tax officers
12. State secretariat service
13. State police and fire brigade services
14. State prison service

There are so many other services in the states, but the distinguishing feature is that unlike USA, the officers of all the services are all selected on merit; they have to qualify in the combined examinations (unlike USA where they are picked up individually by agencies); they all have fixed pay scales, their designations are fixed, and their retirement age is fixed by the state government.

Disciplinary and conduct rules are laid down by the state government. As an affirmative action, reservations are made in all the services for the scheduled caste, scheduled tribes, other backward classes, and now, in some States, also for the economically weaker section of society.

Normally, all states tend to follow the personnel policies laid down by the Government of India. Both the central and state governments have also set up administrative tribunals to decide cases in which there is a dispute on service matters between the Civil servant and the State / Central Government.

Local Government

Each state of India has in each of its district, two types of local bodies; the village councils call the panchayats/ gram sabhas, and the other are the urban local bodies known as municipality's /corporation/ town areas. These urban bodies were created when the British were ruling India. On the other hand, the village bodies had been in existence for several millenniums in one form or the other.

USA has no village structures like India has, but the urban local bodies are more or less of the same genre. It would be worthwhile to study these institutions as they were given constitutional status in 1992.

Panchayats (village committees)

The panchayat system envisages representative government at three levels

- At the lowest rung is the gram sabha and the gram panchayat.
- At the highest level is the district panchayat.
- At the intermediate level is the intermediate Panchayat between the district Panchayat and the village panchayat in state where the population is more than

20 lacs. With lesser population the intermediate level is not mandatory.

Gram sabha is the name for the body of persons who are registered in the electoral rolls relating to a village. Gram panchayat is the elected executive of the village. It is elected directly by the villagers. Thus, democracy percolates to the lowest level.

Each Panchayat continues for five years from the date of its first meeting. The state legislature has the power to confer on the panchayats such powers and authority as may be necessary to enable them to function as an institution of self-government. This power may be with respect to:

- Preparations of plan for economic development and social justice.
- Implementation of schemes for economic development and social justice.
- Matters listed in the Eleventh schedule.

The Eleventh schedule contains 29 entries. Some of the important ones are agriculture, land improvement and soil conservation, minor irrigation, animal husbandry, fisheries, social forestry, village industries, housing, drinking water facilities, roads, education, markets and fairs, health and sanitation, etc.

It may generally be said that Panchayats maintain cleanliness in the village, look after roads, culverts, wells and tanks, establishing drinking water facilities, maintain school and libraries, make arrangements for village affairs and provide famine and food relief. The panchayat has the responsibility to run panchayat enterprises and to maintain watchmen. It has to register births, deaths and keep others statistics.

At the intermediate and district level panchayats, the role is to advise the government in development issues and supervise the work of development officers, chief executive officers, etc.

The finances of panchayats come in the following ways:

- By imposition of taxes as may be permitted by the state act.
- Assignment of Taxes, tolls, fees, etc. collected by the State Government.
- Funds allotted to development activity by the Central / State Government.

At the village /panchayat level there are two main functionaries. One is the village level worker (VLW), a multipurpose functionary, devised under the community development program. Agriculture claims most of the time of the VLW but a set of these workers remain with the block, which is an administrative unit to co-ordinate work of various field departments, headed by the Block Development officer (BDO) and his team of additional Development officer (ADO). Other set of VLWs, under special agricultural programs, are functional in nature.

The second functionary works with the village panchayat. Each village panchayat has a secretary appointed and paid for by the government. Panchayat jurisdiction varies from state to state but roughly two panchayats, constitute the jurisdiction of a VLW. Wherever jurisdictions are small, one secretary has more than one Panchayat under his charge. The panchayat secretary or gram Sevak, as he is also commonly called, is not merely an office worker. He is in charge of Panchayat records but he is also a field worker.

The panchayat is a unit of democratic deliberation and development administration at the grass root level. They participate in the decision-making process about schemes, namely their locations, beneficiary selection and monitoring. They are the recommending authority for planning at the higher level of the panchayat (village body) committee. In this process, the panchayat secretary has a significant supporting role. He is a superior guide for overall development activities unlike the VLW. However, his basic qualification and training does not include the need to be a specialist.

The Blocks

The Block is the established unit of planning and development administration. It has played a key role in the community services and forming an interface with the farmers. The blocks were established as a part of the planned development during the fifties. The blocks have an average of around hundred villages and about 70,000 people under their administrative charge. Every block has an average of 10 VLW's used to assist it in closer interaction with the village community. The

Block Development officer (BDO) is the bureaucratic head, with about a dozen matter specialists. Most of the BDO's remain non-technical coordinators and belong to state cadres. The block has stabilized as the most critical unit of development planning and grassroots delivery system of development, social welfare and other services.

The Districts

The district stands at the head of development administration in the field. Its foundation, in the times of the British, lay in revenue administration that brought regulatory government to the homes of practically every rural family. The district magistrate is the most powerful Civil servant. He is the eyes and ears of the government. All schemes of the government, whether rural or welfare oriented is executed through him. He coordinates between all the agencies and sorts out inter-agency problems.

Together with the Superintendent of Police he ensures maintenance of law and order. Under the Police act enacted by the British, the District Magistrate is the head of the criminal administration of the district. Under him he has officers called additional district magistrates, sub divisional magistrates, the city magistrate and the tahsildars, who assist him in carrying out his functions. The district magistrate also holds court for revenue matters or for minor criminal offences.

He is also required to do a lot of touring to ensure proper maintenance of land records and also to ensure general well-being of the public.

The Municipalities

There was a paradigm transformation of the constitutional system in India. Earlier, The Constitution was only related to the governance of the Union and the states, but the 73rd and 74th amendments made it a three-level system with well-defined jurisdictions within a constitutional framework. The 74th amendment of the Constitution provided the basic framework for legislation to create local self- government institutions for urban India. Municipal committees and Municipal corporations, which were existing prior to this amendment, were made constitutional bodies with the revised mandate. Municipalities are of three types:

- Nagar Panchayat for an area in transition from rural area to an urban area-generally with population between 10000 to 20000.
- Municipal Council for a small urban area, generally with a population between 20000 and 300000.
- Municipal Corporation for a larger urban area- generally with the population exceeding 300000.

Each municipality is divided into territorial constituencies known as wards; members of the municipality are chosen by direct election from such constituencies.

In schedule 12 are listed the matters in regard to which powers may be conferred on municipalities because these are core areas of their functioning. They include urban planning, land use, construction of buildings, road and bridges, water supply, public health, fire services, slums, parks, gardens, playgrounds, Street lighting, parking, etc.

The municipalities have the following sources of revenue:

- Taxes, duties, toll and fees etc. which is the municipality may be authorised by the state legislature by law to levy;
- Texas, duties etc. that are levied and collected by the state but are assigned to the municipality;
- Grants-in-aid to the municipality from the consolidated funds of the state.

For running this municipal bodies, a large staff is recruited. Most of these recruitments are done through the State public service commissions. There are several cadres included in the local bodies' services. The executive part of municipal administration is looked after by the municipal officers and other permanent employees. In the corporations, the municipal commissioner is the executive head, and all other departmental officers like engineers, finance offices, health officers, etc. function under him/her control and supervision.

In a large Corporation like Delhi or Mumbai, the commissioner is usually an IAS officer. In municipalities, the executive officer holds a similar position and looks after the overall administration of a municipality.

Cantonment Boards

They are established for municipal administration for the civilian population in the cantonment areas (the areas where military forces and fruits are permanently stationed). They are set up under the provisions of the Cantonment Act 2006 by the central government and work under the Defence Ministry of the Central Government. The military officer commanding the station is the ex-officio president of the board. The executive officer of the board is appointed by the central government.

State and Local Administration in Usa

The migration from the European countries, Viz. Portugal, Spain and later Britain, offer a unique study of human settlements and their systems of governance. On the face of it, the colonization of America and subjugation of India and a large part of Africa could appear to be similar, but it really differed in each context. The similarity was only limited to the extent that like India, the British had occupied vast areas of North America and its eastern coast through private enterprises or corporates. In case of India, it was ruled by a corporate, East India company (EIC) for 150 years. It's 30-35 directors had obtained authority from the House of Commons to raise an army, and sign treaties. The East India Company influenced British politics. On the other hand, North America was colonized from the 17th century onwards. Most of the migrants were British, but they allowed other Europeans to settle in the vast new territories of the new world.

The immigration centre at New York, which wears a deserted look now, reminds us how the ambitions and aspirations, lured the people to the new lands. In India, the EIC had raised an army and engaged local population to manage its expanding Empire. Its purpose was basically to obtain raw material and ensure capital markets for England's sub-standard post-industrial revolution productions of textiles and other consumer goods. EIC also used Indian land for raising cash crops such as tea, opium and indigo. The British company could be called the pioneer of the business in narcotics, which helped it in controlling China.

The purpose of occupying the new world in America was different than the occupation of India and the Far East. The New World offered vast lands for settling the growing population of England and Europe. Unlike India and China, the indigenous people of North America did not have a sound system of governance. They could not effectively challenge or resist the colonizers. The settlers, the Europeans had enjoyed self-governance. The vast Atlantic Ocean discouraged the governments in Europe to interfere in their routine functioning. There was initially little control from governments back in Europe. Many settlements begin as shareholder or stockholder business enterprises and full governmental authority was vested in the company itself though the British King remained the legal sovereign.

The settlers, owing to the necessity of guarding themselves against the local Indians and wild animals, and to their desire to attend the same Church, settled in small compact townships, or communities which they called towns. The town was a legal corporation, a self-governing political unit, and was represented in the General Court. It was a democracy of the purest type resembling the city state of the ancient Greece and India respectively. The basic difference between a democratic and totalitarian system is that while democracy allows an inbuilt system to make corrections and adjust to the common people's aspirations, in a totalitarian regime, the inadequacies in the system are seldom addressed on the basis of debate and interactions. The towns became the cradles or nurseries of modern American democracy. Several times a year, the adult males met in town meetings to discuss public questions, to lay taxes, to make local laws, and to elect officers.

The chief officers were the "selectmen", from three to nine in number, who would be responsible for general management of the public business, including supervision of the town clerk, treasurer, constables, accessors, and overseers of the poor.

After the Revolution, the electorate chose the governing council in almost every American municipality, and state governments began issuing municipal charters. The townships and County governments and city councils shared much of the responsibility for decision making, which varied from state to state.

The tenth amendment to the US Constitution makes local government a matter of state rather than federal law, with special cases for territories and the District of Columbia. As a result, the states have adopted a wide variety of systems of local government. The categories of the local government established as per the Census of government are as follows:

- County Governments
- Town or Township Governments
- Municipal Governments
- Special purpose local governments

The County governments

County governments are organized local governments authorized in State Constitutions and Statutes. Counties and County equivalents form the first tier of the administrative divisions of the states. All Counties, however, do not have organized County governments. County governments have been abolished in the States of Connecticut and Rhode Island and some parts of Massachusetts. In areas lacking a county government, services are provided by lower level Townships or municipalities or the State itself.

Town or Township Governments

Town or township government are organized local governments, authorized in the state constitutions of 20 North Eastern and Mid-western States. They are established to provide general government for a defined area, generally based on the geographical subdivision of a county. Depending on the respective state laws and local circumstances, a township may or may not be incorporated, and the degree of authority over local government services may vary accordingly to cater to local needs.

Municipal Governments

The municipal governments are organized local governments authorized in State constitution and state statuses, established to provide general government for a defined area, generally corresponding to a population centre, rather than one of a set of areas into which a county is divided. Municipalities range in size from the very small with only one resident to the very large like New York City with more than 8.5 million people. The municipal governments are usually administratively divided into several departments, depending on the size of the city.

Special Purpose Local Governments

These special purpose local governments include school districts. They are organized local entities providing public, elementary and secondary education, which, under State law, have sufficient administrative and fiscal autonomy to qualify as separate governments. The people's participation in school education in states like New Jersey could inspire even developing countries like India, where education is either funded by the Union or the State government. The private schools are being run for profit and the religious institutions too, do offer quality education. In New Jersey, the local people pay taxes for running the local schools, and this payment continues even after their children are grown up.

Special Districts

Special districts are all organized local entities, other than the four above. They are authorized by State laws to provide designated functions as established in the district's charter, and with sufficient administrative and fiscal autonomy to classify as separate governments. These districts administrative unit could be compared with the District units of Delhi government's which enjoy much more autonomy than any civic body in India.

Unlike the relationship of federalism that exist between the U.S. federal Government and the state (in which power is shared), municipal governments have no power except what is granted to them by the states. In India, the oldest municipal committee was set up in Madras. It was constituted in 1688, and was believed to be an attempt to clip the powers of the then governor of Madras Elihu Yale. Earlier, the civic affairs were managed either by the governor or through the agents of the EIC. It was also empowered to levy taxes on the residents for setting up schools, a town hall and even jails. It could also adjudicate on petty matters. Initially, it was constituted with the representation of the English, Scottish, French, Portuguese, and Indian mercantile communities. In North America, the civic bodies too evolved on the same pattern, though the state governments could place whatever restrictions they chose, on their municipalities. The state constitutions which allow counties or municipalities to enact ordinances without the legislature's permission, are said to provide Home rule authorities to the local bodies.

The Governing Bodies

In most cases both counties and municipalities have a governing council, governing in conjunction with a mayor or president. Alternatively, the institution maybe of the Council manager government form with a City manager running the administration, under the direction of the City council.

Census of Local Government

A Census of all local governments in the USA is performed every five years by the US Census Bureau. The last census for which figures are available showed as follows:

Governments in the United States

Type	Number
Federal	1
State.	50
County.	3034
Municipal (city, town, village--)	19,429
Township.	16,504
School district	13,506
Special purpose (utility, fire, police etc.)	35,052
Total.	87,576

Growth of bureaucracy in the states and local governments

Over the last twenty-five years, state and local employment has been growing in scope and scale alike. It could be attributed to the growing needs of the citizens and their expectations from the government. While variations exist in state by state comparisons and across local jurisdictions, Government employment at the state level grew by 35% overall and local government employment increased by over 48% in the previous decade However, the 2009 great recession took its toll on the number of state government workers due to budget cutting, but the process of recovering cut positions has begun. Variations exist across state governments as far as the ratio between citizens to state employees is concerned, but the ratio has decreased from approximately 62:1 in 1982 to 58:1 in 2004. At the local level, the ratio declined from roughly 25:1 in 1982 to 21:1 in 2015. For individuals considering employment at the state and local level, the trend indicates that employees have ----on average----- greater time per citizen, thus increasing the probability of greater personal attention and increased effectiveness.

The proportion of women in state and local employment has increased from 41% in 1981 to nearly 58% in 2015. An analysis of the growth in state and local employment reveals that the increase is mostly in the strength of part-time workers and volunteers. For example, in many states, people volunteer to serve the firefighting outfits. They are trained to handle a disaster caused by fire or any other natural calamity. It enables a small team of the firefighter department to seek the help of common volunteers in the case of such a challenge. In India and China, we should learn from the American experience.

The flexibility engendered through managing part time workers, in essence, brings workers into the workplace on the basis of specific needs only. In India, a department is constituted originally for a specific purpose, but it is retained to keep a large staff employed. The philosophy of the successive popular governments in India has been that it was the duty of the state to create jobs. It has dwarfed Indian economy. Instead, the government should be empowering people under the regulatory umbrella of level playing ground for each citizen. The economic reforms, though pursued vigorously, helped India to survive and grow. The weakening of the state-owned business enterprises in India is a living example of the state's assuming too much role in the economy.

Thus, the success of USA maybe attributed to the emphasis on increasing organizational efficiency. In addition to the growth of part time employment, what is also noticeable is that private sector contractors play a much larger role in state and local government works in USA. In some cases, private contractors have taken over the functions of government previously managed by full or part-time state and local Government employees.

Recruitment of civil servants in the States

The national federal government represents not more than a third of all public jobs. Two third of the public positions are in the City, County and state governments.

New York passed a Civil Service Act in 1883. Till March 1845 only 21 States had done so. The rest followed much later. However, in some cases only a minor fraction of the employees are covered under the law Many cities, especially those with the City manager form of government, practice the merit system although it may not be required by law.

A number of states include their cities, under the civil services, on a state-wide basis. New York and Ohio are examples. In other states, such as New Jersey and Maryland, municipalities can come under the state civil service on their own initiative. Only a handful of County governments have a civil service and less than a dozen have the "manager plan" where by, a well-paid professional manager runs the administration of the government under the policies of the elected County Council or the civic board.

Also, it is possible to start in government service without specific skills or knowledge. If one is a General college graduate, he may take the junior professional assistant examination in the state services, which use such a test. If he passes and is certified, he can take on the job training for a large number of Administrative and technical vocations.

The government jobs in the State can be categorized as follows:

1. Administrative
2. Professional, scientific and technical
3. Clerical

4. Skilled trades
5. Unskilled

The administrative group runs all the way from the non-political man at the top of the departments and bureaus to the personnel, budget, methods and information technicians and administrative aids and assistant at the bottom. School graduation is desirable but is no longer essential to apply for the posts at the lower level. People with training in business administration, economics, economic geography, statistics, accounting, public administration, or similar field have opportunities for jobs in almost every government department and agency.

Only a fraction of the jobs are clerical, although the number is large. The biggest single contingent in the clerical cadre is made up of typists, stenographers and secretaries. This channel is one of the best ways for young women to enter government service.

To get a government job, the first thing to do is to address a letter to the appropriate civil service authority and ask for information about the kind of job you are qualified to do. You will be sent an application form, which one has to fill up and return. Then when the time comes, you will be advised where the examination you have to take, will be held. Also, the US Employment Service has all the information of public jobs.

The respective civil service commissions are the agencies through which the selections are made, if the criteria are merit.

Relations between National, State and Local Governments

As states and communities define their roles, determine benefits from cooperation, and seek outcomes, organizational leaders and state and local professionals, interstate compacts with clear vision and facilitative skills have formed intercommunity partnerships, public private partnerships and other mechanisms for experimentation and implementation. The intergovernmental management system has, in many respects shifted from the vertical domination of the national government to horizontal relationships among local and state governments. At the same time, a more competitive federalism with rival and opposite interests, is also emerging, especially in the area of economic development. Demands for increased governmental efficiency and effectiveness translate to the necessity to develop new and better ways to ensure managerial and governmental accountability. Increased citizen activism thrusts elected officials into more policy activist roles, necessitating greater public administrator skills to do the public's business.

During the period, between the 1950's and the 1970's, the state governments not only reformed their structures and processes but were transformed by court decisions on re appointments (e.g. Baker vs. Carr), which reduced the rural urban imbalance of state legislatures, and the enactment of national civil rights laws, which made it acceptable to think about a serious state role. As state modernization continued into the 1980's, the general public and political elite's support for an increased state role has also developed.

The federal aid as a percentage of state and local government revenue continues to decline. Budget driven federalism, especially federal aid cuts and their "fend-for-self" effects at the state and local levels also instituted cutback management and productivity improvement at the local levels. Subnational governments, however, had to respond to a staggering array of additional responsibilities and new demands. Just as many state programs of the 1920's were models for the national government's New Deal programs, States, in the 1970's and 1980's increased their management capacities and revenues to become the engines of innovations for such policies as education, welfare and the environment. New roles for forged in state-local and state-local-private relations. The intergovernmental lobby grew in skills as did the nation's capacity to understand intergovernmental affairs.

The new public demands for state action seem endless-product liability, the right to die, teenage pregnancy, surrogate motherhood, pay equity, homelessness, AIDS, drugs in school etc. The state and local bureaucracy, together with the politicians, responded well to tackle these challenges.

The states have become domestic policy innovators in such areas as environment and natural resources policy, economic development, health care and human services, education, business and insurance regulation. The states have roped in experts and professionals to come forward with new policies in these areas. States have the relative luxury, compared to National governments, of experimenting with service delivery options. The successes could be retained and failures discarded with minimal risk. The states have proven to be more responsive than the federal government in some policy areas and more cooperative with their local governments then in the past. One result is an emerging analytical consensus within the new policy triangles that is producing leadership, in the direction of a sorting out of government functions across the intergovernmental system. Officials are examining key and separate elements of governmental responsibility: which levels perform a particular function, which controls performance and which pays the costs.

Rather than focusing only on privatization alternatives, a comprehensive look at what government does and many way things can be done is being continuously examined. New forms of intergovernmental cooperation are especially popular, like joint purchasing, circuit riders etc. National agencies at the federal level have been advised to take into account federalism principles and policy making criteria in the formulation and implementation of agency policies.

A national Advisory Commission on Inter Governmental Relations poll of 1989, on public perceptions, asked which government level spends money the most wisely, which responds best to needs, and which has the most honest officials and needs more power. The local governments were rated highest by citizens on all factors and received at least twice as many favourable responses as the national government on each item. The states were ranked second in responsiveness and spending decisions. The national government ranked last on all item except for honesty, for which it ranked slightly higher than state governments. (In India, it might be just reversed. The local bodies, except in Gujarat, are being identified as dens of corruption). Similarly, most of the citizens in USA considered the state administration less efficient than the union government.

There is a growing emphasis on the need to professionalise bureaucracy at the local level. The paradox of professionalism appears to be driven by the reactions to the national government and its bureaucracy. At the local level, citizens are more likely to experience well run governments that facilitates collaborative civic authority and coordinated, institutionalized administration. This is the case specially for council-manager government, in its attempt to practice transformational politics through professionally expert administration that offers relatively neutral access and responsiveness.

State and Local Administration in China

China comprises of 22 provinces (States), 5 autonomous regions and four government controlled municipalities (Beijing, Chonqing, Shanghai and Tianjin). Hong Kong became a special administrative region in 1997, and Macau achieved this status in 1999.

China is a one-party state, with the real power lying with the Chinese communist party. The country is governed under the constitution of 1982 as amended in 1993, the fifth since the accession of the Communist Party in 1949. The unicameral legislature is the National People's Congress. Despite the concentration of power in the communist party, the Central government's control over the provinces and local government is limited, and they are often able to act with relative impunity in many areas.

There are 1355 counties in mainland China out of a total of 2851 County level divisions. Counties are the third level of the administrative hierarchy in Provinces and Autonomous region and the second level in municipalities. In Hainan, a level that is known as County level also includes autonomous counties, cities, banners, autonomous banners and city districts (Banners were administrative and military divisions).

Governors of China's provinces and autonomous regions and Mayors of its centrally controlled municipalities are appointed by the central government in Beijing after receiving the nominal consent of the National People's Congress. The Hong Kong and Macau special administrative region have some local autonomy since they have separate governments, legal systems and basic constitutional laws, but they come under Beijing's control in matters of foreign policy and national security, and their chief executives are handpicked by the central government.

Below the provincial level there are 50 rural prefectures, 283 prefecture level cities, 374 County level cities, 852 County level districts under the jurisdiction of nearby cities, and 1636 counties. There are also 662 cities (including those incorporated into the four centrally controlled municipalities), 808 urban districts and 43002 58 township level regions.

Counties are divided into townships and villages. While most are run by appointed officials, some lower level jurisdictions have direct popular elections. The organs of self-governing ethnic autonomous areas (regions, prefectures and counties)—people's congresses and people's governments—exercise the same powers as their provincial level counterparts but are additionally guided by the law on Regional Ethic Autonomy and require NPC standing committee approval for the regulations they enact.

While operating under strict control and supervision by the central government, China's local governments manage a relatively high share of fiscal revenues and expenditures.

As of 2009, China had about 10 million civil servants who are managed under the Civil Service Law. Civil servants are not necessarily members of the Communist Party, but 95% of civil servants in leading positions from division (county) level, and above, are Party members.

❑

CHAPTER 8

Recruitment of Civil Servants In India, USA and China

Recruitment of Civil Servants in India

Under article 315 of the Constitution of India, it is stated that there shall be a Public service commission for the Union and a Public Service Commission for each state. If two States decide to have a common Public Service Commission than the legislature of the two States will pass resolutions to that effect and then parliament may pass a law accordingly.

The Chairman and other members of the Public Service Commission shall be appointed by the President in case of the Union and the Governor in case of the states. 50% of the members will be from those who have held office for at least 10 years either under the Central Government or under the State Government. This ensures that persons with administrative experience will be manning the Public Service Commission.

The constitution also limits the tenure of the member of the commission, which is a maximum of 6 years or till the member attains the age of sixty-five.

Article 320 of the Constitution lays down the functions of the Public Service Commission, its states:

1. It shall be the duty of the Union and State Public Service Commission to conduct examination for appointments to the services of the Union and the services of the States.
2. It shall also be the duty of the Union Public Service Commission, if requested by any two or more States so to do, to assist those states in framing and operating schemes of joint recruitment for any services for which candidates possessing special qualifications are required.
3. The Union Public Service Commission or the State Public Service Commission, as the case may be, shall be consulted:
    a. on all matters relating to methods of recruitment to civil services and for civil posts
    b. on the principles to be followed in making appointments to civil services and post and in making promotions and transfer from one service to another and on the suitability of candidates for such appointments, promotions or transfers.

c. on all disciplinary matters affecting a person serving under the Government of India for the government of state in a civil capacity, including memorials or petitions relating to such matters.

d. on any claim by or in respect of a person who is serving or has served under the Government of India or the Government of a state or under the Crown in India or under the Government of an Indian state, in a civil capacity, that any costs incurred by him in defending legal proceedings instituted against him in respect of acts done or purporting to be done in the execution of his duty should be paid out of the consolidated fund of India, or as the case may be, out of the consolidated fund of the state.

e. on any claim for the award of a pension in respect of injuries sustained by a person while serving under the Government of India or the Government of a State or under the Crown in India or under the Government of India or under government of an Indian state, in a stable capacity, and any question as to the amount of any such award.

It is clear that the government servants both in the Centre and the State are fully protected from any whimsical order of the Government. The annual reports of the public service commission of the centre and the state are to be presented to the President or the Governor as the case may be. These reports are then sent to the parliament and the State legislature with the acceptance or non-acceptance of the recommendations made.

To give adequate protection to the members and to ensure their independence, it is provided in the constitution under article 317, that the President and members of the Commission can only be removed by an order of the president or the Governor after an enquiry by the Supreme Court.

Our founding fathers realised that to preserve a democracy, it is essential that the permanent civil servants are appointed solely on the basis of merit. The founding fathers did not approve of the spoils system in which a number of civil servants are appointed on considerations of their affiliation and support to the political party in power. In a large country like India which has linguistic, caste and religious divisions, where the government is the largest employer, and where people attach power and prestige to government service, it is all the more necessary to ensure fair play in recruitment to maintain unity of the country and efficiency of administration. Reservation of vacancies in favour of certain classes of citizens (scheduled castes, scheduled tribes and other backward classes) has the approval of the constitution. To provide an instrumentality, which will be a body of experts and which will work independently in a just and fair manner, withstanding pressure and influence, the constitution created the Public Service Commissions.

The Union Public Service Commission comprises a chairman and 10 members. The UPSC makes recruitment for All India Services (the IAS, IFS and the IPS), Group 'A' Central Civil Services/ posts, and Group 'B' gazetted post in Ministries/ Departments of the Central Government. The union Commission also conducts the examination for recruitment of commissioned officer in the defence forces.

The services for which recruitment is made by the UPSC are;

1. Indian Administrative Service
2. Indian police service
3. Indian Foreign Service
4. Indian Post and telegraph accounts and finance Service, Group A
5. Indian audit and accounts service Group A
6. Indian revenue service (income tax) Group A
7. Indian revenue service (customs and Central excise) Group A
8. Indian defence accounts service Group A
9. Indian ordnance factories service Group A
10. Indian postal service Group A
11. Indian civil accounts service Group A
12. Indian railway traffic service Group A
13. Indian railway accounts service Group A
14. Indian railway personnel service Group A
15. Assistant security commissioner in railway protection force Group A
16. Indian defence estates service Group A
17. Indian information Service (junior grade) Group A

18. Indian trade service Group A
19. Indian corporate law service Group A
20. Armed forces headquarters civil service Group B
21. Delhi, Andaman and Nicobar Island, Lakshadweep, Daman and Diu and Dadar and Nagar Haveli service Group B
22. Delhi, Andaman and Nicobar Island, Lakshadweep, Daman and Diu and Dadar and Nagar Haveli police service Group B
23. Puducherry Civil Service Group B
24. Pondicherry police service Group B

The recruitment is done by a combined UPSC civil services examination held every year. The examination is attempted by about half a million candidates each year.

The examination is conducted in three phases:

- Prelims
- Main exams
- Interview

The extent of work being done by UPSC can be gauged from the fact that in any one year, the commissions receives a total of approximately three million (30,00000) applications, and more than 9000 candidates are interviewed for civil services/ posts. A total of more than 600 candidates are recommended for appointment to various post in one year.

Another recruiting agency of the Government of India is the Staff selection commission to make recruitment in group B (non-gazetted) and Group C (non-technical) posts in the Government of India. The staff selection commission has also been assigned the additional responsibility of making recruitment to group B (gazetted) post of Assistant Accounts Officer and Assistant Audit Officers for the Indian audit and accounts department. The commission makes its recruitment through two models i.e. all India open competitive examination for filling up regular vacancies and secondly through selection method for recruitment to isolated post in various Ministries/ departments.

Pay Structure of civil Servants in India

Since 1956, the pay structure of civil servants under the central government, have been fixed through the Pay Commission set up every 10 years. The pay commission is an administrative system to review and make recommendations on the work and pay structure of all civil and military divisions of the Government of India.

Government jobs are high paying jobs as compared to private sector jobs. The pay commission keeps all the monetary needs of an employee in mind. Apart from the basic salary, pay commissions determine the dearness allowance to be paid to compensate for the cost of living; travelling allowance, house rent allowance etc.

Further there are benefits for working in harsh condition. For instance, a soldier or a civilian working in the snow-clad mountains gets extra monetary benefits for working in harsh terrains, or a government doctor who is not practicing, gets a non-practicing allowance. There are several benefits for working women as well. A pregnant woman gets paid maternity leave. Government employees also get an education allowance to meet partially the cost of educating their children (upto two).

The Pay Commission also makes recommendations on the pensions and allowances to be given to retired employees of government services. There are hikes in pension along with the regular salaries for the retired employees. The State government subsequently set up their own pay commissions, which mutatis mutandis follow the recommendations of the central ay commission for the State Government employees as well as the employees of the local body's i.e municipal corporations, town areas etc.

The pay Commission also fixes the minimum and maximum pay scale for government servants. Secretary to the Government of India gets ₹ 2,25,000 per month while the minimum pay is ₹ 18,000 per month. Prior to this, in the sixth pay commission, the minimum salary was ₹ 7000 per month and the maximum salary was ₹ 80,000 per month.

Government servants also get official residences at subsidised rates. Where official residences cannot be provided, the government servants get house rent allowance, which is quite substantial.

Professionalism in the Civil Services

In almost every part of the world, attacks against bureaucracy have reached new peaks of intensity but are often little more than rationalizations for a persistent drive to arrest and reverse the historical process which led to the development of the administrative state. Such attacks call into question two fundamental concepts that have been at the centre of civil service reforms for close to two hundred years: neutrality and professionalism in the service of the State.

Professionalism in the Civil Services in India and USA

India has one of the world's most complex and developed public service system. In the 18th and 19th centuries, it served as the laboratory for the British to experiment with new ideas that were later to become the bulwark of not only the British system but also of most British colonies. India adopted the parliamentary system of governance. It is exactly in contrast to the American presidential system, where the executive power is purposefully concentrated in a single office.

Even though the Indian political system is modelled after the British, its administrative system is a hybrid of the British legacy and its own social and cultural heritage. The historical factors also had a bearing on bureaucratic development. In 1947, when the partition took place both the countries were settled with the same type of bureaucracies, which existed under the erstwhile British India. In Pakistan, the army generals grabbed power, but in India, the parliamentary system was retained with regular elections.

In 1994, Fred W. Riggs, the famous public administration expert, concluded that American bureaucracy harbours an exceptional degree of professionalism and that this professionalism is responsible for the stability of the American presidential system.

Presidential and parliamentary systems are inherently different. Most industrialized countries are parliamentary in the sense that their political power is not separated into compartments of executive, legislative and judiciary. The United States is in contrast, a presidential system with clear separation of the three as given in the US Constitution.

Most of the former British colonies have some form of parliamentary system, while the countries under the influence of the United State resemble the American presidential system. In the last 50 years, a significantly larger number of presidential and parliamentary system have been taken over by military rules or dictatorships. Parliamentary systems have a greater degree of resilience and able to sustain stable democracies.

One of the most important internal challenges to a political system comes from its bureaucracy (Riggs). Bureaucracy over a time period, becomes more knowledgeable, gathers more expertise, becomes more cohesive, and more assertive. Often, it becomes the single most organised organisation. Although curbing the ambitions and power of such an organisation is a daunting task, parliamentary system, due to its single most important characteristic, that is consolidation of political power, is more capable of controlling such a bureaucracy than its presidential counterpart is. The parliamentary system is more cohesive and can provide a unified front to counterbalance bureaucracy's power. In other words, one can say that cohesiveness in a parliamentary system (concentration of all powers in the hands of the prime Minister) helps in preventing the growth of a parallel bureaucratic power system. This is not to say that bureaucrats are not powerful in a parliamentary system, like in India, but they are. They, however, are unable to become dominant enough to develop their own independent political agenda.

Riggs says that "Amongst representative governments, those that set a fixed term for the head of government like the USA are much more vulnerable to break down via a coup d'état, then are regimes, in which a governing cabinet is subject to discharge by a no confidence legislative vote (i.e. parliamentary regions having fused executives/legislative powers). This may be explained by the greater capacity of parliament regimes to maintain control over their bureaucracies and, as a result to sustain higher administrative performance level so that both public officials as well as the general public are more likely to trust them and voluntarily respect their authority.

India

India is a constitutional parliamentary Federal democracy with clearly defined roles of each institution. The political system in India is a modified replica of the British system, nonetheless, there are three important differences that give it an independent character. These differences are critical for the organisation and functioning of the bureaucracy. First, unlike Great Britain, India does not have a two-party system. It has at least eight national parties that contest and win elections in more than two States, and a long list of Regional parties. Despite this, the country was governed by the Congress party for the major part in the initial years. Now of course, other national parties like the Bharatiya Janata party (BJP) with its coalition partners have come in the forefront. In a way, we might call it the two grouping systems, i.e. the National Democratic Alliance (NDA) and the United Progressive Alliance (UPA). In a parliamentary model, the two-party system / group plays an important role. Because all the powers are concentrated in a single office of the prime Minister, some internal check on this office is necessary. The opposition party /group, which in a two party /group scenario is almost parallel in strength, serves this very function.

The Indian political system is Federal, in contrast to the British system; it must accommodate the priorities and needs of the 29 states and 9 Union territories. States in India have a separate social and cultural identity and are often eager to assert it. This leads to a very complex environment for the bureaucracy, for it must absorb the pressures coming from various directions: the Centre, the State and the socio-economic interactions amongst the States.

Another factor to be taken care of is the judiciary. The Judiciary in India is relatively independent. The constitution gives the Supreme Court the right to review all laws. The Supreme Court also entertains Public interest litigation and often passes orders which the Government is compelled to follow. The Supreme Court is intervening in matters of financial policies which used to be earlier no go matters for the courts.

Federalism in India refers to relations between the Centre and the States of the Union of India. The Constitution of India establishes the structure of the Indian state. Part XI of the Indian constitution specifies the distribution of legislative, administrative and executive powers between the union government and the States of India. The legislative powers are categorised under a Union List, a State List and a concurrent List, representing, respectively, the powers conferred upon the Union government, those conferred upon the State governments and powers shared among them.

At the same time, power in India is not as fragmented as it is in the United States. The Union Government has several means to control the states. The Prime Minister also has the power to recommend appointment of state governors. This power becomes particularly important when state legislatures are controlled by the opposition.

The role and character of the Indian bureaucracy was compatible with the needs of the political system at the time of the British. In fact, the administrative system worked so well that Indian leaders decided to adopt it without modification after getting independence in 1947. Applauding the role of the bureaucracy, Sardar Patel the first Home minister of independent India stated; "I wish to place on record of the house that if during the last two or three years, most of the members of the service had not behaved patriotically and loyalty, the union would have collapsed... You will not have a United India, if you do not have a good All India Service which has the independence to speak out its mind, which has a sense of security that you will stand by your word".

Thus, in the Indian Constitution adopted in 1950, the place of the bureaucracy was not only preserved but also glorified. According to article 311 of the constitution (mentioned earlier), a Civil servant cannot be dismissed, without a show cause notice. Organizationally there are several layers and sections of the bureaucracy. The Indian Administrative Service (IAS) at the apex of organisation, provides leadership and vision. This is the elite group of civil servants who are placed at all—federal, state and local levels of key administrative posts. The overall rate of growth in the Indian bureaucracy parallels the growth in other countries.

Earlier, the majority of the IAS recruits came from the urban areas but with the opening of coaching centres, a large number have qualified from the rural areas too. The candidates can opt for giving their examination in any of the language recognised by the Constitution; therefore, the elitist English-speaking candidates no longer rule the roost as before.

However, the elitist nature of the civil services, especially of the IAS remains. This elitism causes alienation in India. It has resulted in feeling of mistrust and aloofness among subordinate bureaucrats. This has adversely affected the public perception of bureaucracy. Bureaucrats are viewed as maladjusted, lacking in dedication, often corrupt and authoritarian. In fact, people of all classes and regions, consider it a past time, to share horror stories of their bureaucratic encounters.

According to Samuel J Eldersveld (He was an American academic, political scientist, and Democratic politician who also served as Mayor of Ann Arbor, Michigan from 1957 to 1959), the urban, educated, high class people distrust public administrators more than the rural poor and uneducated. There was a large presence of freedom fighters during the first three decades after 1947. The country's politicians, irrespective of their political ideology, were committed to the welfare of the common people, but in contemporary India, each political party has a large number of legislators accused of heinous crimes. In this backdrop, it is not an uncommon practice, even for politicians, to blame bureaucrats in public. This negative public image necessarily counterbalances the power of the Indian bureaucracy.

Most of the Indian bureaucrats having been good scholars during their students' days. They remain aloof from the masses. For many it is an elitist orientation. They are less likely to get involved in public affairs or politics. Maybe they lack the mass appeal necessary to be able to create a following or to organise opposition to a politician, but still they are trusted and if they are victimized, the media and common people take up their cause. However, in many developing countries there are cases when the Civil servants challenge the political bosses.

Oath of Neutrality

The civil services in India are expected to be neutral. They implement the policies of the party in power without being a part of it. The Central Civil services conduct rules, forbid a government servant to be a member of or otherwise associated with any political party or campaign directly or indirectly for the ruling party. However, it is possible that family members of the Civil servant may be functionaries of a political party. Apart from not being a part of a political outfit, it is also expected from the Civil servant to prevent every member of his family from taking part in, subscribing in aid of, or assisting in any other manner, in movements or activity, which is directly or indirectly deemed to be subversive of the state.

The Civil servants can vote to their preferred political party, but cannot campaign for it. In recent years, there are number of cases, when the bureaucrats contested elections following their superannuation. The present foreign minister, Subrahmanyam Jaishankar and Hardeep Singh Puri, Minister of State for Urban Development, have served in the Indian Foreign Service and have immaculate records. They have also excelled as Ministers in the current government.

Earlier, the Swatantrata party, launched by C. Rajagopalachari, the first Indian governor general of India, following the departure of Lord Louis Mountbatten in 1948, had attracted a large number of top civil servants, who were for free economy. They included CG Desai, HM Patel and Lobo Prabhu. During the Congress regime, Kunwar Natwar Singh, a Foreign Service official, decided to join the Congress party. Yashwant Sinha, who had started his political innings with Chandrashekhar (a former Prime Minister) in the Janata party, later joined the Bharatiya Janata party. He served as Union finance minister during the tenure of Prime Minister Atal Bihari Vajpayee. The former Union home secretary, RK Singh, contested elections after his superannuation. He is presently serving as minister of state for power (independent charge) in the Narendra Modi government.

Since 1952, as many as 17 general elections for the Lok Sabha, the lower house of bicameral parliament have taken place in India. The governments changed, but the political and administrative system, under the supervision of the Civil servants, maintained neutrality. It enabled the new political order to assume responsibility, and serve the country. The transfer of power from one party or coalition to another has been smooth. Furthermore, it provided continuity and stability in a system where politician's terms are unpredictable. In India during the years of chaos (the time of partition in 1947), political turmoil (emergency years from 1975 to 1977), and leadership uncertainty (following Indira Gandhi and the Rajiv Gandhi's assassination in

1984 and 1991 respectively), it was the bureaucracy that held the country together through its iron grip.

It is quite natural to ask to questions, firstly, how this neutrality is assured and secondly how the political and bureaucratic differences on a given issue, may, is resolved. These issues have drawn attention of experts also in the context of the recruitment system. The Civil servants in the IAS and allied services are appointed for life based on their exceptional performance in a set of written and oral examinations. They are groomed to take up responsibilities in the higher echelons of the administration. Maybe, this is the reason why even today, Indian bureaucracy is respected for its in-depth understanding and competence. Pakistani military dictator, Pervez Musharraf, in his book mentions that he was able to persuade prime Minister Atal Bihari Vajpayee for a long-term agreement on the issue of Kashmir, but due to the objection of a senior Foreign Service official, Vajpayee declined to sign the Accord.

The Constitution protects our civil services from arbitrary dismissal and removal from service. There has always been recognition of their merit and commitment to work. There was an earlier tradition to announce the superannuation of a senior Civil servant that he has demitted office instead of it being stated that he has retired. This tradition has been discontinued.

With a view to keeping the image of the services before the common people, the senior officials were never abused, or faced allegations. Even in case of any grave irregularity, the senior officials would be quietly reprimanded and may be asked to quit if the enquiry officer finds him guilty. Once, the wife of an ICS officer complained to Jawaharlal Nehru that her husband was involved with her sister. Nehru summoned the official and took his resignation, but it was seldom discussed in the public domain (It is about Balkrishna Rao, an ICS of the UP cadre).

According to the provisions of the constitution, the All India Service officers are appointed by the President of India, and can only be removed in consultation with him and the UPSC. This ensures that if the officers want to remain politically neutral, as required by the Civil Service conduct rules, they can do so.

Professionalism in the Indian Bureaucracy

The Identity of the Indian bureaucracy lies in its mandarin, generalist nature. There is much emphasis on non-partisan judicious approach in governance. The Civil servants take an oath of commitment to the Constitution, and constitutional provisions provide norms and conditions for their behaviour in public. Unlike the United States, where civil servants are bound by the norms and standards of their individual professions, the primary norms and standards for Indian Civil servants are laid down in the Civil Service regulations. It is expected that upon joining, bureaucrats will put these standards before any other professional obligations and will draw their strength and charter from them.

The term professionalism in India has a specific meaning. The term professionalism encompasses the ideas of neutrality, sincerity and integrity. It implies a dedicated service to the people, the promotion of welfare and happiness of the citizens and respect for the feeling and susceptibility and principles of fairness and integrity in all his dealings. Being professional, thus means being beyond the norms and conditions of all narrow subject disciplinary vested interests, whether engineering law or medicine.

This particular notion of professionalism is accepted and promoted in India through various means. The administrative part of public administration was almost reserved for people coming from the liberal arts background, particularly from history, economics or political science.

In general, till the sixties, physicians and lawyers were expected to serve in their respective fields. That meant that they would remain devoted to their professions and be specialists instead of undertaking administrative responsibilities. However, the situation started changing during the Indira Gandhi regime. Amidst the reports from various departments of bungling in funds, she shifted the financial power from the departmental heads in the district, to the district collector. Even in the State Government medical Colleges, the payments were finally sanctioned by the department of health Under Secretary. The bills were cleared only after paying a substantial amount of money to the powers-that -be in the system. A large number of infants had died due to the non-supply of oxygen to the medical College hospital in Gorakhpur. The oxygen supplier was not paid money despite a number of reminders, because he had reportedly declined to pay bribe to the high-ups, including the Minister in the government.

With the centralisation of financial power and nexus between the corrupt bureaucrats and politicians, many professionasl were prompted to abandon their hard-earned professional qualification to join the Administrative Services. The rampant corruption and harassment of the professionals, prompted many of them to abandon their respective field to join the civil services. They also felt that if they have to work under the IAS, it is better to join the service to "wield the real power of the government". A large number of them started appearing in the All India Service examinations. They might not have been satisfied with their technocratic status, but many among them, perhaps, became more miserable in the services. A few years ago, a district collector of Kanpur used to go quite frequently to the IIT, Kanpur, either to study a specific issue or feel at home with the academic environment.

In India, in terms of hierarchy, technocrats, despite their specialised knowledge and expertise are placed below generalists holding administrative positions. Many getting huge salaries in the corporate abandon their high profile jobs, to become even a state civil service official.

The young men and women having technical qualifications could get opening in the government jobs as engineers or doctors. There is no need to qualify for the IAS, but when they realised that the real decision makers were the IAS officers, they started yearning for this position of power, though the country needed these professionals for development. But with the centralisation of power, there is a clear movement towards the generalist cadre of the civil services, whether it be the IAS, IPS, IFS or the allied Central services. The technocrats felt that becoming an administrative officer and wielding power over all departments is much better than staying at a subordinate position.

Thus, one finds that professionalism as defined in the United States could not take roots in a democratic India. During their long tenure, Nehru and Indira Gandhi introduced draconian licensing systems and levied high taxes on the corporate. Maybe, it suited them politically. Donations from corporates to the political parties were also banned. It increased the role of black money in politics.

During 1990s, when the Narsimha Rao led government started dismantling this control regime, it was noticed that most of the Indian corporate were just dwarfs and could not compete with the foreign companies. Earlier, the top scientist and technologists had migrated to USA, but those who stayed back in India were relegated and hardly had any voice in policy making. Even after three decades of the opening of the economy, India is still a bureaucracy driven country. During the era of promotion of public sector, India became the dumping yard of the obsolete technologies. Thousands of technically skilled people work in the public sector, but they are marginalised in the process of decision making and administration.

The role of the civil service is to act as a trigger to the economic activities and development, but they have been pushed to the cesspool of power rivalries. In the government, like a human body, each body part has a specific role. The movement of the technocrats towards the unending lane of administration is a national loss.

Tecnocrats adhere to the norms and standards of the civil services more readily than they do to the norms and standards of their specialised professions. They considered this necessary to serve the public and to satisfy the demands placed on them by their generalist supervisors.

Riggs argues that it is because of this non professionalism in the Indian bureaucracy that they offer a unified identity. On the other hand because of the high level of professionalism in the American bureaucracy they do not offer a monolithic identity whereas a unified bureaucracy is necessary for cohesion in policy making.

But another aspect that is worth considering as far as Indian bureaucracy is concerned, and which prevents the internal cohesiveness which is apparently there externally, are several factors- social, cultural, and political. The social political culture of India affects the administrative culture. The two factors—caste and religion, are particularly important to bureaucratic disposition. According to R B Jain, a well-known political analyst, it leads to dysfunctionalism, by promoting unhealthy practices like sons of the soil and authoritarianism.

The caste issues entered the civil services in India in 1940s when government decided to create a quota for the underprivileged castes. Emerging as a temporary solution, caste-based quotas became a permanent condition. In past decades, quota size has increased. An additional quota was created by the VP Singh government for backward classes and later even for the economically poor upper classes. Though the Supreme court has declared that quotas cannot exceed 50%, but under pressure, various States beat the restrictions by subterfuge. This has created a feeling in the higher castes, of being discriminated against because (A) entrance criteria for reserved seats are lower and (B) because competition for the seats is less fierce. These feelings have left a permanent scar. At the very least, they are prohibiting bureaucrats from developing a unified identity. The government organisations are marred by caste identities.

Other than caste, religion in India also undermines the emergence of a unified identity amongst officers. Because the Indian Civil servant works in a milieu full of social and religious fervour, his behaviour necessarily becomes culture bound or else he risks social disapproval. Although there are no reserved seats for religious minorities, religious identities certainly effect bureaucratic behaviour (Dwivedi and Jain).

There is thus a forceful influence of social factors on bureaucratic practices (Khator). There are specific ways in which social preferences find expression in administrative decision making. Bureaucratic discretion was often used to kill policies in favour of the social elite (whether they were religious leaders, fellow caste persons, or people belonging to the economically privileged class). In social forestry for instance, a study found that seeds and sapling distributed free of charge under a World Bank program, went mostly to upper caste farmers (Khator). Social preferences were asserted through bureaucratic discretion, available in the form of transfer and promotion of junior officials.

According to Dwivedi and Jain, "when the upper caste assume bureaucratic office, their aim is not merely to expand their ranks through favouritism, but also to invest their caste values with the quality that they consider will be acceptable to other caste and communities".

Thus, although lack of professionalism exists in India, it does not have a decisive impact on the bureaucracy. It has not been conducive to the development of a single identity because of the complexity of Indian society. The divisive forces of society have their reflections on the bureaucracy too.

Recruitment of Civil Services in USA

The US Civil Service Commission was first created on March 3, 1871, when President Ulysses S. Grant signed into law the first civil service reform legislation, which had been passed by Congress. The Act created the United States Civil Service Commission that was implemented by President Grant and funded for two years by Congress lasting until 1774. However, Congress members, who relied heavily on patronage, under the Spoils system, especially the Senate, did not renew funding of the Civil Service Commission. President Grant's successor, President Rutherford B. Hayes requested a renewal of funding, but none was granted.

President Haye's successor, James A, Garfield, advocated Civil Services reform. His efforts against the spoils system, (also known as patronage) were cut short after he was assassinated by a job seeker, Guiteau.

Pendleton Law

President Garfield successor, President Chester A. Arthur, took up the cause of civil service reform and was able to lobby Congress to pass the Pendleton Civil Service Reform Act in 1883. The Pendleton law was passed in part due to public outcry over the assassination of President Garfield. The Pendleton Act renewed funding for the Civil Service Commission and established a three-man Commission whose Commissioners were chosen by President Arthur.

The Civil Service Commission administered the civil service of the United States Federal Government. The Pendleton law required applicants to take the civil service exam in order to be given certain jobs; it also prevented elected officials and political appointees from firing civil servants, by removing civil servants from the influences of political patronage and partisan behaviour. President Arthur, and succeeding President's, continued to expand the authority of the Civil Service Commission and the number of Federal Departments that the Civil Service covered. The Civil Service Commission, in addition to reducing patronage, also alleviated the burdensome task of the President of the United States in appointing federal office seekers.

Under the commission model, policy making and administrative powers were given to a semi-independent Commission rather than to the President. Reformers believe that a Commission formed outside the President's chain of command would ensure that civil servants would be selected on the basis of a merit system and the career service would operate in a politically neutral fashion.

Civil Service Commission typically consisted of three to seven individuals appointed by the chief executive on bipartisan basis and for limited terms. Commissioners were responsible for the direct administration of personnel system, including rulemaking authority, administration of merit examinations, and enforcement of merit rules.

The 1978 reorganization

Effective January 1, 1978, functions of the commission were split between the Office of Personnel Management and the Merit Systems Protection Board under the provisions of the Reorganisation Plan 2 of 1978 and the Civil Service Reform Act of 1978. In addition, other functions were placed under the jurisdiction of the Equal Opportunity Commission, the Federal Labour relations authority and the Office of Special Counsel.

Employees Strength

According to the office of personnel management, there were more than 2.8 million civil servants employed by the

US Federal Government, which included employees of the departments and agencies run by any of three branches of government (the executive branch, legislative branch, and judicial branch and the 600000 employees of the US postal Service).

There are three categories of US Federal employees

- The Competitive Service includes the majority of civil service positions, meaning employees who are selected on merit after a competitive hiring process that is open to all applicants.
- The Senior Executive service (SES) which is the classification for non-competitive, senior positions filled by career employees or political appointments (e.g. cabinet members, ambassadors etc.).
- The Excepted Service includes non-competitive jobs in certain Federal agencies with security and intelligence functions.

Each government entity is responsible for its own employment system, takes care of its own personnel needs and engages in different hiring practices. There are more than 105 hiring authorities in existence at present in the Federal government.

Office of Personnel Management

The mission of the office of personnel management is "recruiting, retaining and honouring a world-class force to serve the American people". It is responsible for maintaining independence and neutrality in the administrative system.

While technically employees of the agencies they work for, Administrative Law Judges are hired exclusively by the Office of Personnel Management (OPM), effectively removing any discretionary employment procedure from the other agencies. The OPM uses a rigorous selection process which ranks the top three candidates for each Administrative Law Judges vacancy and then makes a selection from those candidates, generally giving preference to veterans.

The OPM is also responsible for a large part of the management of security clearances (National Background Investigations Bureau conducts these investigations) for the US government. With the exception of the Nuclear Regulatory Commission, which maintains its own system, separate programs for each executive department have gradually been merged into a single, government wide clearance system. The OPM is responsible for investigating individuals to give them Secret and Top-Secret clearances.

OPM is also responsible for Federal employee retirement applications for FERS and CSRS employees. OPM makes decisions on Federal employee regular, and disability retirement cases. OPM also overseas FEHB and FEGLI, the health insurance and life insurance program for Federal employees.

The OPM also takes its fees for service rendered. It takes money from the various Federal agencies for Human Resource Services.

In July 2013, the Office of Personnel Management Inspector General Act was enacted, to increase oversight of the fund that was created by the fee collection of the OPM for services rendered. This act ensures funding of the expenses for investigation, oversight activities and audits from the OPM revolving fund.

Merit System Protection Board

The merit systems protection board is an independent, quasi-judicial agency in the executive branch of US administration that serves as the guardian of Federal merit systems. The board was established by reorganization plan number 2 of 1978, which was codified by the Civil Service Reform Act of 1978 (CSRA). The CSRA, which became effective, from January 11, 1979, replaced the Civil Service Commission with three new independent agencies: office of Personnel Management, Federal Labour Relations Authority (FLRA), which oversees Federal labour-management relations' and the MPSB.

The MPSB assumed the employees' appeals functions of the Civil Service Commission and was given new responsibilities to perform merit system studies and to review the significant actions of the Office of the Personnel Management (OPM). The civil services Reform Act 1978 also created the office of special counsel (OSC), which investigates allegations of prohibited personnel practices, prosecutes those who violate Civil Service rules and allegations, and enforces the Hatch Act. Although originally established as an Office of the Merit Protection Board, the OSC now functions independently as a prosecutor of cases before the board (MSPB).

The mission of the MSPB is to protect the merit system principles and promote an effective Federal workforce free of prohibited personnel practices. MSPB's vision is, "A highly qualified, diverse Federal workforce that is fairly and effectively managed, providing excellent service to the American people. MSPB's organisational values are excellence, fairness, timeliness and transparency. MSPB carries out its statutory responsibilities and authorities primarily by adjudicating. In addition, MSPB reviews the individual employee appeals and by conducting merit system studies. In addition, the MSPB reviews the significant actions of the office of personnel management (OPM) to assess the degree to which those actions may affect merit.

Discrimination

The United State constitution prohibits discrimination by Federal and state governments against their public employees. Federal law prohibits discrimination in a number of areas, including recruiting, hiring, job evaluations, promotion policies, training, compensation and disciplinary action. State laws often extend protection to additional categories of employers.

The Fifth Amendment to the US Constitution mandates due process to be followed in every action of the government. This due process protection requires that Government employees have a fair procedure process before they are terminated, if the termination is related to a "Liberty" such as the right to free speech or property interest. Some state civil rights laws offer protection from employment discrimination on the basis of sexual orientation, gender identity or political affiliation.

Under Federal laws, employers generally cannot discriminate against employees on the basis of race, sex, pregnancy, religion, National origin, disability either physical or mental, age, genetic information, bankruptcy or bad debts.

Salary and Pay Structure of US civil Servants

The pay system of the United States Government civil service has evolved into a complex set of pay systems that include principally;

- General schedule (GS) for Blue collar employees
- Senior executive system (SES) for executive level employees
- Foreign Service schedule (FS) for members of the foreign Service

Apart from the above mentioned, there are more than 12 alternate pay systems that are referred to as alternate or experimental pay systems. The current system began as the Classification Act of 1923 and was refined into law with the Classification Act of 1949. These Acts that provide the foundation of the current system have been amended through executive orders and through published amendments in the federal register that includes approved changes in the regulatory structure of the Federal pay system. The aim of the government is to achieve the goal of paying equitable salaries to all involved workers, regardless of group, system or classification. This is the principle of pay equity ("equal pay for equal work"). Selected careers in high demand, may be subject to a special rate table. These careers include certain engineering disciplines and patent examiners.

The general schedule (GS) includes white-collar workers at level 1 to 15, comprising mostly professional, technical, administrative and clerical positions in the federal civil service. The federal wage system for wage grade (WG) schedule includes most Federal blue-collar workers. Over 70% of Federal civilian employees were paid under the general schedule (GS); the remaining 30% were paid under other systems such as the Federal wage system for Federal Blue-collar employees, the senior executive service/ senior level/and the executive schedule for high-ranking Federal employees, and the pay schedules for the United States postal service and the Foreign Service. In addition, some Federal agencies such as the United States Securities and Exchange Commission, the Federal Reserve System, and the federal deposit insurance have their unique pay schedules.

All the federal employees in the GS system, receive a base pay that is adjusted for a locality. Locality pay varies, but is at least 10% of base salary in all parts of the United States.

Nineteen percent of Federal employees earned salaries of $ 100000 or more in 2009. Most menial or lower paying jobs, have been outsourced to private contractors. GS salaries are capped by law so that they do not exceed the salary for executive schedule IV positions. The increase in civil servants making more than $150000 resulted mainly from an increase in Executive schedule salary of rules approved during the administration of George W. Bush, which raised the salary cap for senior GS employees slightly above the $150000 threshold.

The Federal government is the nation's single largest employer. Almost all Federal agencies are based in the Washington DC region. However, this accounts for only about 16% of the Federal government workforce. In 2016, women made up more than 43% of the Federal executive branch work force.

Civil Service Retirement System in USA

The Civil Service retirement system (CSRS) in USA was organised in 1929 and has provided retirement, disability, and survivor benefits to most civilian employees in the United States Federal government. Upon the creation of a new Federal employees retirement system (FERS) in 1987, those newly hired after that date, cannot participate in CSRS. However, CSRS continues to provide retirement benefit to those eligible to receive them. CSRS is a defined benefit plan, akin to a pension. Notably though, CSRS employees do not participate in social security.

Employees hired after 1983 are required to be covered by the federal employees retirement system (FERS), which is a three tiered retirement system with the smaller defined benefit (pension), social security and a 401(k) style system called the thrift savings plan (TSP). The defined benefit of both the CSRS and the FERS systems are paid out of the Civil Service retirement and disability fund.

With changes in the determining retirement coverage of Federal employees under FERS or CSRS, those employees who are later rehired and were covered under CSRS, will retain their CSRS coverage, if they meet certain service rules. In general, if rehired civilian employees have five years of civilian service left, they will retain CSRS coverage.

Public Employees' pension plans in the United States

In the United States, public sector pensions are offered at the federal, state and local levels of government. They are available to most, but not all public sector employees. These plans may be defined benefit or defined contribution pension plans, but the former have been most widely used by public agencies in the US throughout the late twentieth century. Some local governments do not offer defined benefit pension but may offer a defined contribution plan.

Pension plans may or may not be changed after an employee is hired, depending on the State and the plan. The retirement age in the public sector is usually lower than in the private sector. The public pension plan managers in the United States take higher risk in investing the funds then one outside the United States, or those in the private sector

Recruitment of Civil Services in China

In traditional China, it was Confucianism that prevailed in the management of bureaucracy. Confucianism, especially during its last five countries, became the main administrative doctrine of a political order that was largely bureaucratic in character. The imperial government under the Chinese emperors, had a clear hierarchy of offices, a formal system of ranks, and substantial structural differentiation, particularly at the centre and provincial levels. Confucianists also recognised the need for a large body of formal laws and organisational regulations.

Confucianism recommended recruitment on the basis of moral qualifications, not technical competence. Moral norms were superior to formal rules and regulation which were to be overridden in the case of conflict. This philosophy held that Government by regulation could only be adjunct to the informed judgement of officials, whose education was firmly grounded in the ethical teachings of the past.

The Confucian principles of government were institutionalized in the Civil Service examination that most of the, would be officials, had to pass, in order to enter government service. Success in the examinations required not knowledge of techniques of administration, but lengthy study of the Confucian classics, which emphasised moral rectitude, personal abnegation and service to society- (Harry Harding). The examinations were rigorous and competitive, and in time came to reward style of writing and beauty of calligraphy more highly than clarity of thought, and to prize normative judgement more highly than simple adherence to regulations.

A professional corps of dedicated bureaucrats, akin to a modern civil service, has been an integral feature of governance in Chinese civilization in much of its history. It was emperor Wu of Han (141-87 BC) who standardised the selection process with the addition of question and answer elements on classic texts judged by a panel of scholars. This helped lay the groundwork for the imperial examination system that was widely adopted thereafter.

During the revolution and after 1949, the Communist Party's recruitment policy had emphasized on political commitment rather than technical skills for intellectual ability. Most of its members lacked administrative experience. Though there were some 4.5 million party members at the end of 1949, only some 7, 20,000 were minimally qualified to serve as party cadres or as government officials.

The party recruited its new carder from four groups: young graduates of middle school and universities, older non-party intellectuals and technical specialists, selected officials from former Nationalist Government and mass activists. In addition, it also sought to retrain veteran party members in required technical, administrative and cultural skills, so that they could be promoted to administrative positions.

By the end of 1952, these channels for recruiting new officials and retraining veteran party members had gone a long way towards alleviating the cadre shortage of late 1949. In September 1952, it is reported, that the party had been able to recruit 2-6 million new cadres since 1949. Adding to the 7,20,000 cadres already available to the party in 1949, the new regime now had some 3.3 million officials on the job. In 1956, all government and party employees were occupying one of the 30 ranks (the upper 26 for administrative grades, the lower for clerical service grades).

Party organisation departments at the Central, provincial and County levels were given the responsibility of making appointments to administrative posts in the party. Together with the Party communities and Party branches inside the state bureaucracy, they also maintained the files of all government personnel who were party members, assigned Party members to positions in the government, and supervised the work of the state personal apparatus. A parallel system of state personnel agencies—consisting of the ministry of personnel (renamed The Bureau of personnel in 1954), the provincial and County personnel departments, and the personnel sections with government Ministries and departments were formally responsible for the appointment, promotion, transfer, dismissal and punishment of all government officials. In practice, however, state personnel agencies deferred to the party in the management of party members and in the selection of important government officials.

In August 1952, the central authorities were given control over the allocation of college and university graduates. In 1956, similar control over the assignment of technical specialists were given to a Central Bureau of experts. Throughout the period the central personnel organs made or approved all appointments of County magistrates and party first secretaries, all provincial appointments above the level of bureau director, and all Central Government and Party appointments above the level of deputy Bureau Director. This meant in fact that all cadres in the 213 grades of the 26 grade salary structure for administrative cadres were directly controlled by personnel agencies in Peking (Beijing).

The State administration of civil services was created in March 2008 by the National People's Congress. It is under the management of the ministry of Human resources and Social Security. The function of the administration covers management, recruitment, assessment, training, rewards, supervision and other aspects related to Civil Service affairs. The administration also has several new functions. These include drawing up regulations on the probation period of newly enrolled personnel and the registration of civil servants under Central departments.

Civil servants in China are recruited now through an open examination. Candidates will need to take a national written exam for general jobs, while those applying for positions related to finance, public security, foreign affairs and other specialised fields have to give an additional professional skill test. Candidates are then evaluated based on their overall performance in the written tests, a physical examination and an internship.

Political integrity is a primary criterion and the majority of the positions in party and government agencies, above the provincial level will require 2 years of grassroot work experience. Certain requirements, such as test scores and work experience, are lowered for those applying for positions in remote poor areas. About 9,20,000 people took the national civil examination in 2018.

❑

CHAPTER 9

A Comparative Study of Civil Services of India, USA and China

"Mirror, Mirror on the Wall; which is best bureaucracy of all".

We have made an extensive study of the evolution of bureaucracies in democratic countries like India and USA, and also seen how bureaucracy developed in an autocratic country like China, better known as the People's Republic of China (PRC). All the three countries, including China, boast of having democratic institutions. All of them assert that they have elected representatives, who decide on policies and enact legislation. While USA conventionally has a two-party system, India has more than 1200 registered political parties, though the parties that fight elections at the national and state levels would be less than hundred. On the other hand, China only has a one-party system. With some new changes, the democratic system, promised to the people of Hong Kong, too, has been forcefully ended. The freedom of press has ended. All the three countries have written constitutions, but only USA and India have an independent judiciary. In China, the judiciary is manned by political cadres.

China's system has been defined officially, as the dictatorship of the proletariat. The present-day rulers in China cannot be called as dedicated as their predecessors, who had fought for years, amidst the deep forests for the people.

Under the one-party rule of the Chinese communist party, voices and protest are being muzzled. The Communist party's tentacles have gripped all the organs of the government. Any new leadership has to grow within the party and not outside. The press is controlled tightly. The Civil servants are also selected not only on merit but loyalty to the party. The ecosystem therefore is completely different in China as compared to USA and India.

The bureaucracies in all these three countries can be justifiably proud of the services they have rendered to their countries. While USA is the most technologically and economically advanced nation of the world, China has over the years become the second most economically strong country after USA and it boasts of a formidable military might. India is the leading economic power in the emerging world, and also has the third largest standing army among all the Nations. Bureaucracies in all these three countries, together with their political leadership, have played an important role in bringing these countries to the forefront in the global order.

A study of the strategies adopted by the governments of the three countries in dealing with the pandemic of coronavirus will show the strength and weaknesses of their respective joint politico bureaucratic structure.

In India, the fight against coronavirus was led by the medical experts as well as the generalist bureaucracy. Three elements of the system, i.e. the political leadership, bureaucracy and the professionals i.e. doctors were on the same page. The Union and the State government's response to the pandemic-symbolised in bureaucratic orders, guidelines and clarifications- were shaped by a complex decision-making bureaucratic process. It, invoked key Union Ministries and sectoral experts, inputs from state governments, intensive analysis of data, an assessment of daily reports and finally approval of the Prime Minister. These guidelines had the force of law. There were two main laws which gave strength to these guidelines, namely the Disaster Management Act of 2005 and the Epidemic Act of 1897. These two acts are stringent enough, with no major legal obstacles. Under the Disaster Management Act, the Union government could issue orders or directions to the entire country, while the State government could issue for the entire state and the District magistrate for his district. The district magistrates could also punish anybody who disobeys their directives, including orders like wearing of masks. This they are allowed to do under section 188 of the Indian Penal code. Thus, in India, the bureaucrat's role became much pronounced to steer the country out from the crisis.

Ever since the lockdown, the regulations issued by the Ministry of Home affairs have regulated the lives of citizens, defined the scope of economic activities to be allowed, enabled or prohibited transport of vehicles. Whenever, a new situation arose during the Covid-19 crisis, like that of stranded migrant workers, the Ministry of Home affairs (the nodal ministry for the Disaster Management Act of 2005), the health ministry and Indian Council of Medical Research got together, to formulate guidelines.

Since the states were also to be taken on board, a parallel process was institutionalized with the Cabinet secretary convening meetings with State governments, where many key secretaries are also present. The government also listened to the viewpoints of other stakeholders, particularly those involved with the economy. Every aspect of the guidelines were discussed threadbare at different levels. Between the NDMA (National Disaster Management Authority), chaired by the Prime Minister and the Ministry of Home affairs, discussions on the finer aspect of the guidelines, used to take place. Finally, only after the PM gave his nod, the guidelines were issued. The Prime Minister depended a lot on the advice given by sectoral experts and inputs from the States.

The ongoing fight against coronavirus threw up several instances of local initiatives and empathy on the part of the Civil servants. The Bhilwara, Agra and Pathanamthitta (Kerala) models of containing virus became world famous.

Several health care officials and doctors falling prey to coronavirus, while leading the fight against it, were inspiring evidence of their selflessness and empathy. In several States, IAS officers, who joined government after doing MBBS (medical graduation) did an excellent job in persuading the citizens to follow the safe distancing protocol and other precautionary measures.

In spite of a democratic structure of governance, the Indian bureaucracy showed that the Indian state's coercive arms could be strong and efficient. The locking down of an entire nation of India with its size and diversity, was no easy task. But the fact that all the security arms of the State came together, from the centre to the state and from the state to the districts, and enforced this lockdown is a testament to the fact that when the State wishes to implement something on a large scale, it can do so even in a liberal environment with an intelligent bureaucracy.

The live interaction between the government and the people throughout the crisis helped in the effective management of the pandemic. The daily briefing of the press and other media was done by senior bureaucrats. The public was kept informed of the spread of the coronavirus in India, and steps being taken to counter it.

In USA, the total number of deaths due to the coronavirus far exceeded the total number of deaths in the Vietnam War. The US government did not heed the advice of its medical advisors to have a lock down and prevent people from mixing. Each state took its own decision. In the initial period it was only the governors of California and Washington who ordered their residents to stay at home. The Tennessee administration permitted its restaurants to open. Pennsylvania State government decided to do unlocking in three stages. Thus, no uniform policy could be followed. This was also because the Federal government did not have any legislation in place which would enable it to issue directions to the states. Though the Institute for health metrics and evaluation recommended wearing of masks to reduce the spread of the virus, the administrations, both at the federal and state level refused to act in uniformity. The political approach in dealing with the pandemic weakened the efforts to prevent its spread. The Democratic Party run States, such as New York and New Jersey, imposed strict social distancing measures, while the Republican states like Texas and Florida rushed to reopen businesses. The pandemic was treated as a State and local issue. There was no standardised Federal intervention on the pandemic. The governors and local officials were made responsible for handling it. As a result, the approaches and results varied considerably from state to state. It was left to the state to source medical equipment and supplies and also to arrange for the testing. The states had to acquire these from overseas or private sources.

The Federal government appointed Vice president (VP) Mike Pence to head a task force to advice on what to do but gave it no real authority. The Vice President's task force developed guidelines for states and localities for testing, tracking and treatment of the virus; and the use of mask and social distancing to prevent its spread. However, these remained as guidelines, not enforceable under any law. The task force held regular briefings until the country began to reopen.

The lack of a uniform enforcement mechanism, lead to chaotic handling of the situation. The extent to which states enforced sheltering at home, wearing of masks and social distancing varied sharply. In some States, such as Georgia and Texas with Republican governors and large cities with democratic Mayors, the governor's only recommended actions to fight the coronavirus, while the measures required enforcement by law. Meanwhile, the President and his advisors consistently rejected and discounted expert advice. The suggestions given by the expert in the task force, Dr. Antony Fauci, was rejected repeatedly.

To sum up the US experience, one can say that the bureaucracy, including the medical bureaucracy, could not live up to the challenge of tackling the pandemic, Covid-19, believed to be a biological war. It failed to convince its political masters of the need to have a uniform strategy in fighting the pandemic. They failed in persuading the Federal government to enact legislation which could ensure that the directives of the Federal government are to be followed by all the States whenever such crisis arises.

In China, the authorities first denied the existence and spread of the coronavirus. They in fact, put the scientist, who announced the existence of this virus, in jail. They also tried to persuade the World Health Organisation to play down this crisis. It is only when the virus spread rapidly and deaths occurred, that the Chinese government accepted the existence of the virus and put up strong measures to control it. The entire government machinery got geared up and enforced severe lockdown. Unlike USA, the orders of the Central government in China were strongly enforced throughout China. This could be attributed to the advantage an authoritarian regime, always has over a liberal democracy. But the negative aspect was that reporting of the spread of the virus in the media was controlled in the manner government wanted. This has the disadvantage that incidents of the virus caused deaths, which in a liberal democracy could be brought from promptly to the notice of the government, did not happen.

In fact, till today nobody has any authoritative figure on the persons adversely affected by coronavirus in China and how many died. Since most of the Civil servants and the technical and medical staff are members of the Chinese communist party, they cannot speak out freely. The censorship on the spread of the news is strict. In a large country like China, if the media is free, and can report freely, it could have been an advantage to the government to tackle a crisis before it actually engulfed the country as well as the world.

The scientific experiments being carried out in the Chinese government laboratories is also kept secret. There is no sharing of information. In a globalised world, where knowledge can be pooled to the advantage of the world's population, such secrecy is a great disabling factor.

China has been rightly condemned for this attitude in all the countries. Since the Chinese bureaucrats as well as the Chinese political heads are part of the same Chinese communist party, no independent advice is tolerated or encouraged. This is also a failure of the system.

Controlling Financial Markets in Period of Lockdown

In India, ever since the lockdown was announced, in late March, a team of more than 200 personal from the reserve Bank of India (RBI) and services providers were sent to four locations to ensure that the financial markets and the system works uninterrupted and provides glitch free service to users. The top RBI bureaucrats went into a huddle immediately after the lockdown was announced and a team was set up to ensure that the services are provided 24 x 7 without any interruptions. They worked with some of the best technologies available to keep the systems on despite, the strict lockdown measures. Thus, RBI services continued throughout the lockdown. The RBI Governor incidentally is also a retired Civil servant.

In USA, the Government adopted several stimulus measures to avoid an economic crisis. Payment of unemployment allowances lead to a massive outflow of revenues of the federal government. The markets, which are the parameter of financial health also sank in the initial months. There was often dissonance between the US Federal Reserve Bank and the US government. The US

President was often very critical of the steps and strategies of the US Federal Reserve.

In China though the GDP was negative, but because the economy is completely under the control of the Chinese government, the government tided over the crisis gradually.

The Diplomatic Bureaucracy

Some of the best examples of the bureaucracy in any country are the diplomats who keep their country's flag flying in faraway countries.

In USA, the political masters usually overrule the bureaucracy. So whether it was the agreement with Iran, or the WTO or the WHO, much as the US diplomats would have preferred to continue with the existing policy, they overruled and USA withdrew even from commitments made internationally. The USA under the present regime became isolationist in its approach.

China, because of its strong economy had already spread its tentacles through the belt and road initiative in Asia, middle East, Europe and Africa, It flooded various countries with large amounts of money. However, with the worldwide spread of the coronavirus, its diplomats failed to protect China from the blame that followed. All the nation's felt, that if China had not hidden the fact which emerged from their labs about this virus, perhaps it could have been controlled earlier. USA is boycotting goods made in China and has substantially reduced its trade with China. India is also following this policy. The companies having their origins in China have become suspect. The world is seething with anger and the distrust against China has spread. It only reflects the failure of Chinese diplomacy, notwithstanding its economic clout.

On the other hand, the civil servants in India, manning posts in the Indian Foreign Service, are thorough professionals. They have managed to stall China on various for a, whether it be the United Nations general body or the United Nations Security Council. Though China is a permanent member of the UN Security Council having veto power, our diplomats have succeeded in ensuring action against Pakistan, China's all-weather friend, for its support to the terrorist trained and funded in that country. Pakistan had stalled all action against these terrorists, even though adequate proof had been given against them, for what they did in Mumbai. India found itself helpless in persuading the Pakistan government, which is being prompted by China, to take action against the named terrorist, our diplomat succeeded by adopting the FATF (Financial Action Task Force) route and compelling Pakistan to proscribing these organisations. Indian diplomats also succeeded in ousting the Chinese from Maldives and restoring India's presence on that Island. India has been able to enlist the support of USA and the European nations in the border dispute with China in Ladakh. India has also succeeded in making its presence felt in the South China sea together with USA. It is true that China has made inroads into Nepal and to some extent Myanmar, but here also the Indian diplomats are working quietly.

In spite of the financial crisis, the Indian government continued to give financial aid to almost 64 Nations throughout the world. The aid amounts to 30.66 billion dollars. India has also opened up 300 lines of credit. Under the Indian development and economic assistance program, these countries are being given credit by India at a nominal rate of 1.5% for 15 to 20 years. The countries covered include those in Africa and Asian countries. Aid acts as a strong weapon to expand India's influence and the Indian diplomats have quickly adopted this route.

Similarly, in Bangladesh, China stepped up its Covid-19 diplomacy to the point of taking up vaccine trials in Bangladesh. India highlighted the fact that the Chinese aid came with stringent conditions, whereas Indian aid is not so. Bangladesh had hoped that China would help in bringing up the Rohingya issue to the UN Security Council but this did not happen. Dhaka also knows how isolated Beijing is within the UNSC, while Delhi, having become a non-permanent member of the security council, could actually do much better. The Indian diplomatic machinery acted fast to bring home the fact that Dhaka and Delhi mutually benefit from a shared understanding of their strategic and security environment.

Handling of Coronavirus Crisis in India

The Covid-19 pandemic has swept three fourths of the world. Different countries have reacted differently. But the Indian strategy has impressed the entire world. In spite of the huge population, India has managed to reduce the damage by balancing economic requirement with the necessity of preserving human lives. The political leadership combined with an active civil service showed a path for fighting this crisis in a determined manager using all the resources which this nation possesses, including technology, science, Medical and health research facilities as well as the security establishment.

Rarely has the Indian state been put to test as it was done during the crisis, the central and state governments showed decisiveness in formulating strategies and amending them, based on the feedback received from the States as well as the field. Decision making is difficult in a democracy, which has to contend with multiple interests and voices. Power in a federal structure is fragmented, but the governments remained alert. Despite its weaknesses, (load testing in the initial stages, the slow pace at which it provided personal protective equipment for health workers) the State acted decisively, took a route that it knew would have high economic cost, and stayed the course- largely allowing scientific inputs and data to drive decision making.

All the security arms of the state came together, from the centre to the states and strongly enforced the lockdown. The district magistrates on the field, the civilian doctors, health and sanitation workers laboured hard, day and night, to control the spread of the epidemic. It showed that when the state wishes to implement something on a large scale, curtailing the liberties of citizens for any purpose (in this case for the noble objective of preserving public health) it can do so. Whenever there is a clear directive from the centre, and if the states are on board with it, then the Civil servants including the police, can deliver.

The governments broad response to the coronavirus

pandemic—symbolised in bureaucratic orders, guidelines and clarifications with wide-ranging impact—was shaped by a complex bureaucratic guided decision making process. It involved key Union Minister and sectoral experts, inputs from state governments, intensive analysis of data, an assessment of daily reports, and finally a nod from the Prime Minister.

Ever since the national lockdown was announced on March 24, guidelines by the Ministry of Home Affairs, signed by the union home secretary, have regulated lives of citizens, defined the scope of economic activities to be allowed, enabled or prohibited—transport of persons and vehicles. It was the Civil servants who assessed the prevailing situation everyday and issued orders stipulating a set of relaxations in varying degrees in red, orange and green zones.

Behind the formulation of the guidelines, the officials devised an elaborate process. As a phase of lockdown ended or a new crisis, like that of stranded migrants emerged, the officials of Ministry of home affairs, the health ministry and Indian Council of Medical research would spring into action.

To look after inputs and consultations with the states, the Cabinet Secretary was put in charge. He would convene meetings with the State governments and take their inputs to shape the guidelines. Many key Secretaries were also present. The officials also, together with their ministers, listen to the perspective of other stakeholders, particularly those involved in the economy, and then carefully weigh the trade-offs.

When the guidelines on extending the federal lock down till May 17 was issued, it was preceded by a series of meetings, both formal and informal of the civil servants In one of the video conferences, ICMR made presentations with charts and projections on the rate of the Covid-19 spread, how the virus is likely to progress, the situation in Covid hotspots and how the green and orange zones are faring.

The officials of the Union health ministry, then provided its inputs from the public health perspective. Based on input from the Cabinet secretariat and other sources, the Union home ministry would prepare draft guidelines for further discussion. After the inter-ministerial consultations for over, the issue would be taken up by the National Disaster management authority and the Prime minister's office. Between the national disaster management authority, chaired by the PM, and the Ministry of Home Affairs there were at times some discussions on the finer aspects of the guidelines. The Prime Minister, who was spearheading the national battle against this deadly virus, depended a lot on the sectoral experts and inputs from the States before taking a final call.

It is relevant here to state that the Prime Minister also would directly interact with the field officers like the District magistrate and the Chief Secretaries of states to ascertain field problems and issues. He maintained a balanced outlook between suggestions given by the officers as well as advice given by his political colleagues.

As far as the public face for fighting Covid-19 was concerned the Prime Minister left it to the officers to brief the press and television channels. The Prime Minister felt that the officials who advise him on various aspects of the fight against Covid-19 were the best persons to brief the media. It was indeed a spectacular performance by the officials as they took up their responsibilities knowing that they had the confidence of the Prime Minister and his colleagues.

Lessons to Be Learnt

Future public servants need to be able to create value by combining the ability to collaborate and utilise and disseminate pertinent information efficiently. A balanced vision and an ethical consciousness in responding to the government's role to secure an equitable resource allocation and to act as a growth engine in coordinating market activities are needed. In the years to come, the most successful governments will focus on finding and solving problems outside of government rather than trying to solve social problems themselves. They will build platforms, hold partners accountable for targeted outcomes, open their services to choices and manage crowd sourced campaigns and competitions. In this case, governments will assume the role of solution recruiters.

The talented individuals, who use intelligent technology for government administration and administrative services, are required to skilfully handle and collaborate with machines, while providing the human sensibility and speculation that machines cannot replace. Change is a constant factor in today's public sector. Therefore, public investment in the skill sets that civil servants ought to possess is required for governments to become more nimble, agile and adaptable. In sum, the talent capacity required for future governments will require expertise and collaboration capacity, analytical and combinative capabilities, machine literacy, the ability to speculate and situational judgement.

In the future, efficient communication between civil servants, machines and citizens will be of vital importance. This is particularly true in cases where machines replace routine tasks. Consequently, public servants will have to focus on expanding their ability to communicate based on their emotional capacity and their human intuition—skills that cannot be substituted by a machine.

Ultimately, future public officials should possess greater levels of experience, creativity, sensitivity and flexibility so that they cannot be replaced by robots or machines. In other words, future civil servants should have the ability to utilise machinery in their quest for creative innovation in performing their policymaking and implementation tasks.

The obvious question stemming from the preceding discussion is what talent we should seek in future governments. It seems that considerable diversification and customisation needs to take place in the recruitment and appointment processes, leading to a convergent job-centred recruitment system that aims to locate future talents.

❑

Epilogue

Peace continues to elude mankind even after the end of the World War-II. The erstwhile world power, United Kingdom, conceded the leadership of the free democratic world to USA. Even during the post Second World War II years, spanning a period of almost three decades, peace could not prevail on this earth. The allies of the world war years 1939-45, USA and USSR, became arch enemies. They competed with each other, both in military and economic strength in what came to be known as the Cold War. The West was scared of USSR under Joseph Stalin, with his huge Army fresh, after defeating the aggressive forces of the Axis powers.

On behalf of the free world, colonial India supplied the necessary manpower required by the allied forces. The Indian National Congress, led by Mahatma Gandhi and Jawaharlal Nehru, though opposed to fascism of the German dictator, Hitler, refused to participate in the war efforts. On the other hand, the Muslim league, patronised by the British, supported the war efforts. Almost half a million soldiers were recruited from the undivided Punjab province of British India. Of them two thirds were Muslims. These professional British soldiers trained the

Muslim soldiers, though secular in training, became the top heavy army of Pakistan, following India's partition. With the eclipse of the political outfit, especially, Muslim league, the army took over the reins of the Government in Pakistan. Thus, Pakistan became the most favourite nation of the western powers in the region to resist the communist influence.

During the mid-thirties to 1949, the Communist Party of China (CPC) had launched an armed struggle against the then pro west government in Beijing. The CPC, which was inspired by the Bolshevik revolution in Russia, took over China on October 25, 1949 forcing the incumbent Kuomintang government to take refuge in the Taiwan province.

The outgoing colonial power of the region, UK was apprehensive of the Communist takeover of China. During the signing of the Potsdam treaty in 1945, the then British Prime Minister, Sir Winston Churchill, had told the US President Franklin D. Roosevelt, that India has to be divided to establish a Muslim state loyal to the West. The new state, according to him was necessary to prevent the march of the Communists in the region. Within four years of Churchill's apprehensions shared with Roosevelt, CPC, came to power in China. Indeed, he had a rare foresight.

During the initial years, especially in fifties, China and India were economic pygmies. In spite of becoming the central authority, the CPC had to struggle for next two decades for asserting its position in the UN Security

Council. While China was trying to stabilize against the anti CPC element within the country, India too faced formidable challenges for her existence, though it was the "peaceful transfer of power" from the outgoing colonial imperial power, UK.

Amidst the challenges of her existence, India's "Tryst with Destiny", as India's first Prime Minister Jawaharlal Nehru, told the Constituent assembly of the midnight of August 14-15, 1947, had begun amidst the crisis of partition. The new rulers of the Indian democracy were apprehensive of the two key institutions of colonial India, the Indian Civil Service and the Indian Army. They were identified with repressive regime of a foreign power. They were professionally world class institutions. The army had the experience of the two world wars and even today it is one of the finest institutions in the world. Similarly, India's new journey as an independent nation begins with the dedication of the bureaucracy, which followed the British lineage of commitment to work.

The Civil servants in India with Indian Civil Service (ICS) officials at the apex were serving their motherland with much more dedication to save her nascent independence and democracy. It was reincarnated under the new name, Indian Administrative Service (IAS). There was no dearth of the highly efficient and dedicated officials manning the top positions, both in the Union government as well as the State governments. It has kept the country united and enabled it to meet the formidable challenges of the partition, aggressions and her march to progress. It was the foresight of the founder of the modern Indian state that the constitution ensured independence to the Civil services. The constitutional provisions were incorporated due to the efforts of the visionaries like BR Ambedkar and C Rajagopalachari, who had become Governor General, after Lord Mountbatten. The role of the Civil servants in a democratic polity, was further consolidated by Prime Minister Nehru and the Home minister Sardar Patel. They encouraged to the Civil servants to give their views freely, which enable the country to be benefited by a non-partisan opinion, within the system.

In China, all the public posts were manned by the members of the Chinese communist party or by people who were inclined to be loyal and faithful to the objectives of the CPP. Though periodically, recruitment was made on merit through public examinations, but here also, those selected were expected to follow the policies of the party. The distinction between political heads and the Civil servants recruited through examinations, remained blurred in China. So, in effect, two models of bureaucracy came into being in China and India, during their initial years of their modern existence.

The USA without a similar centralised bureaucratic system has attained and retained the position of a top economic power in the world. During the past half century, China and India have progressed, but India's economic development has not been spectacular.

In 1947, when India gained independence her

population numbered about 340 million. The literacy level then was 12%, or about 41 million people. In 1949, China's population was 540 million and its literacy level was estimated at 20%, or 104 million.

In 2019, India's population scaled to 1.34 billion people and literacy level reached 74% for about 1 billion people. In 2019, China also had a population of about 1.3 to billion people and literacy of 85% or 1.14 billion. Both India and China lifted almost a billion people each, from ignorance of the world to modest knowledge. China employed a highly mobilized and centralised system of government, with no restraints on coercion to achieve this, while India achieved this under a system of voluntary compliance.

In 1947, India accounted for only 4% of the world's GDP. In 2019, India accounts for 8.5% of world's GDP. The savings rate has arisen from eight percent of GDP to 29% and continues to be on an upward trend.

If one factors the human cost in China, India did better. In 1947, India chose to be a full democracy and a nation of equals. It ordained itself to having a government by popular choice with an attendant political economy and all the implied pitfalls. India felt that all aspirations needed to be heard and reconciled, and hence, conceived of a nationality based on shared aspirations, not on shared beliefs.

This was also true of USA and the bureaucracies of both India and USA worked in that environment.

In China however, with the political philosophy of the dictatorship of the proletariat and complete domination of the Chinese communist party, the bureaucracy and the political leadership became a monolith with no freedom to the Civil servants to express their views and be heard. This, of course, enabled China to develop their economy at a more rapid rate, than India. There is no check on executive power in China. Even the judiciary is mostly manned by the cadres of the CPP.

To sum up while USA is a country, more than 240 years old with a dominant economic position in the world, both India and China are young nations with a rich past, trying to position themselves in the international order.

The US bureaucracy is a matured setup, which has grown up facing two world wars and numerous challenges like the Cuban crisis, Depression of the thirties, Vietnam and Korean wars as well as the Lehman crisis. China and India have faced both internal and external threats but both of them have evolved in a comparatively more peaceful environment. The bureaucracy both in China and India has helped their political masters to achieve national stability and rapid economic development.

Out of these three countries, the bureaucracy in India assumes a leadership role and compensates for the political inadequacies. During the colonial years, almost a similar role was expected from the ICS officials.

In USA, the bureaucracy retains its anonymity and it is the political leadership which for all intents and purposes remains on top. In China, because the civil bureaucracy is interwoven in the political leadership of the Chinese communist party, their role in development is less obvious and less discernible. If the role of the civil services is compared, the Indian bureaucracy has successfully proved its effective and prominent role from managing the Covid-19 pandemic to the country's economic and social development, as compared to its counterparts in the other two countries.

In India, unlike the other two countries there have been continuous efforts to reform the bureaucracy. The first Administrative Reform Commission was set up in 1966. The economic and financial reforms of 1991 freed many parts of the economy from direct Government control. Thereafter a second Administrative Reforms Commission was set up in 2005 under Veerappa Moily.

The present Indian Government under Sri Narendra Modi has been experimenting with reforms such as lateral entry and digitisation. The Government has announced the establishment of a National Recruitment Agency to replace the bewildering network of recruiting agencies in Government. The Indian Prime Minister has now announced Mission Karmyogi with the objective of promoting transparency, professionalization and use of technology by the civil servants.

Promoting a creative style of leadership is essential in public service Technological development is a viable way to meet this goal, as assigning repetitive and routine tasks to machines will allow a civil servant to focus on continually developing creative and innovative policies and service models. Furthermore, as machines will eventually approach human abilities level, the value of human spiritual aspects will rapidly increase, requiring redesigning types of leadership. The three elements that a leader needs to possess in order to enhance the creativity of public officials: internal motivation, professional knowledge and experience and creativity skills. Consequently, in the future, the most desirable leadership quality will be the ability to stimulate the internal motivation of employees, for them to demonstrate their creativity.

This type of leadership enhances internal motivation through the existence of a strong organisational mission and makes bureaucracy more effective. Amongst the three countries, India is the only country which is consciously moving towards this direction.

❑

Appendices

Appendix 1: Extracts of the Indian Constitution Relating to Civil Services

Part XIV: Services under the Union and the States

Article 309

Recruitment and conditions of service of persons serving the Union or a State

Subject to the provisions of this Constitution, Acts of the appropriate Legislature may regulate the recruitment and conditions of service of persons appointed, to public services and posts in connection with the affairs of the Union or of any State.

Provided that it shall be competent for the President or such person as he may direct in the case of services and posts in connection with the affairs of the Union, and for the Governor of a State or such person as he may direct in the case of services and posts in connection with the affairs of the State, to make rules regulating the recruitment, and the conditions of service of persons appointed, to such services and posts until provisions in that behalf is made by or under an Act of the appropriate legislature under this Article, and any rules so made shall have effect subject to the provisions of any such Act.

Article 310

Tenure of office of persons serving the Union or a State

1. Except as otherwise provided by the Constitution, every person who is a member of a defence service or of a civil service of the Union or of an all-India service or holds any post connected with defence or any civil post under the Union holds office during the pleasure of the President, and every person who is a member of a civil service of a State or holds any civil post under a State holds office during the pleasure of the Governor of the State.

2. Notwithstanding that a person holding a civil post under the Union or a State holds office during the pleasure of the President, or as the case may be of the Governor of the State, any contract under which a person, not being member of a defence service or of an all-India service or of a civil service of the Union or a State, is appointed under this Constitution to hold such a post may, if the President or the Governor as the case may be, deems it necessary in order to secure the services of a person having special qualifications, provide for the payment to him of compensation, if before the expiration of an agreed period that post is

abolished or he is, for reasons not connected with any misconduct on his part, required to vacate that post.

Article 311

Dismissal, removal or reduction in rank of persons employed in rank of persons employed in civil capacities under the Union or a State

1. No person who is a member of a civil service or an all –India service or a civil service of a State or holds a civil post under the Union or a State shall be dismissed or removed by an authority subordinate to that by which he was appointed.
2. No such person as aforesaid shall be dismissed or removed or reduced in rank except after an enquiry in which he has been informed of the charges against him and given a reasonable opportunity of being heard in respect of those charges. Provided that where it is proposed after such inquiry, to impose upon him any such penalty. Such penalty may be imposed on the basis of the evidence adduced during such inquiry and it shall not be necessary to give such person any opportunity of making representation on the penalty provided. Provided further that this clause shall not apply:
   a. Where a person is dismissed or removed or reduced in rank on the ground of conduct which has led to his conviction on a criminal charge, or
   b. Where the authority empowered to dismiss or remove a person or to reduce him in rank is satisfied that for some reason, to be recorded

by that authority in writing, it is not reasonably practical to hold such inquiry, or

c. Where the President or the Governor as the case may be, is satisfied that in the interest of the security of the State it is not expedient to hold such inquiry.

3. If, in respect of any such person as aforesaid, a question arises whether it is reasonably practical to hold such inquiry as is referred to in clause (2), the decision thereon of the authority empowered to dismiss or remove such person or to reduce him in rank shall be final.

Article 312

All India Services

1. Notwithstanding anything in Chapter VI of Part VI or Part XI, if the Council of States has declared by resolution supported by not less than two thirds of the members present and voting that it is necessary or expedient in the national interest so to do, Parliament may by law provide for the creation of one or more all India services(including an all India Judicial service) common to the Union and the States, and subject to the other provisions of this Chapter, regulate the recruitment, and the conditions of service of persons appointed to any such service.

2. The services known at the commencement of this Constitution as the Indian Administrative Service and the Indian Police Service shall be deemed to be

services created by Parliament under this article.

3. The all-India judicial service referred to in clause (1) shall not include any post inferior to that of a district judge as defined in article 236.

4. The law providing for the creation of the all-India judicial service aforesaid may contain such provisions for the amendment of Chapter VI of Part VI as may be necessary for giving effect to the provisions of that law and no such law shall be deemed to be an amendment of this Constitution for the purposes of Article 368.

Article 312A

Power of Parliament to vary or revoke conditions of service of officers of certain services

1. **Parliament may by law-**

   a. Vary or revoke, whether prospectively or retrospectively, the conditions of services as respects remuneration, leave and pension and the rights as respects disciplinary matters of persons who, having been appointment by the Secretary of State or Secretary of State in Council, to the civil service of the Crown in India before the commencement of this Constitution, continue on and after the commencement of the Constitution(Twenty eight Amendment) Act 1972, to serve under the Government of India or of a State in any service or post.

b. Vary or revoke, whether prospectively or retrospectively, the conditions of service as respects pension of persons who, having been appointed by the Secretary of State or Secretary of State in Council to a civil service of the Crown in India before the commencement of this Constitution, retired or otherwise ceased to be in service at any time before the commencement of the Constitution (Twenty eight Amendment) Act 1972.

   Provided that in the case of any such person who is holding or has held the office of the Chief Justice or other Judge of the Supreme Court or a High Court, the Comptroller and Auditor General of India, the Chairman or other members of the Union or State Public Service Commission or the Chef Election Commissioner, nothing in sub clause (a) of sub clause (b) shall be construed as empowering Parliament to vary or revoke, after his appointment to such post the conditions of his service to his disadvantage except in so far as such conditions of service are applicable to him by reason of his being a person appointed by teg Secretary of State or Secretary of State in Council to a civil service of the crown in India.

2. Except to the extent provided for by Parliament by law under this article, nothing in this article shall affect the power of any legislature or other authority under any other provision of the Constitution to

regulate the conditions of service of persons referred to in clause (1)

3. Neither the Supreme Court nor any other court shall have jurisdiction in:
   a. Any provision in any dispute arising out of any provision of, or any endorsement on any covenant, agreement or other similar instrument which was entered into or executed by any person referred to in clause (1), or arising out of any letter issued to such person, in relation to his appointment to any civil service of the Crown in India or his continuance in service under the Government of the Dominion of India or a Province thereof;
   b. Any dispute in respect of any right, liability or obligation under article 314 as originally enacted.
4. The provisions of this article shall have effect notwithstanding anything in article 314 as originally enacted or in any other provision of this Constitution.

Functions of Public Service Commissions

Article 315

Public Service Commission for the Union and for the States

1. Subject to the provisions of this article there shall be a Public Service Commission for the Union and a Public Service Commission for each State.

Article 320

1. It shall be the duty of the Union and the State Public Commissions to conduct examinations for appointments to the services of the Union and the services of the State respectively.
2. It shall also be the duty of the Union Public Service Commission, if requested by any two or more States so to do, to assist those States in framing and operating schemes of joint recruitment for any services for which candidates possessing special qualifications are required.
3. The Union Public Service Commission or the State Public Service Commission, as the case may be, shall be consulted-
   a. On all matters relating to methods of recruitment to civil services and for civil posts.
   b. On the principles to be followed in making appointments to civil services and posts and in making promotions and transfers from one service to another and on the suitability of candidates for such for such appointments, promotions or transfers.
   c. On all disciplinary matters affecting a person serving under the Government of India or the Government of a State in a civil capacity, including memorials or petitions relating to such matters.

d. On any claim by or in respect of a person who is serving or has served under the Government of India or the Government of a State or under the Crown in India or under the Government of an Indian State, in a civil capacity, that any costs incurred by him in defending legal proceedings instituted against him in respect of acts done or purporting to be done in the execution of his duty should be paid out of the consolidated Fund of India, or, as the case may be, out of the Consolidated Fund of the State:

e. On any claim for the award of a pension in respect of injuries sustained by a person while serving under the Government of India the Government of a State or under the Crown in India or under the Government of an Indian State, in a civil capacity, and any question as to the amount of such award,

f. And it shall be the duty of a Public Service Commission to advise on any matter so referred to them and on any other matter which the President, or as the case may be, the Governor of a State, may refer to them:

Provided that the President as respects the all-India services and also as respects other services and posts in connection with the affairs of the Union, and the Governor, as respects other services and posts in connection with the affairs of a State, may make regulations specifying the matters in which either generally, or in any particular class of case or in any particular circumstances, it shall not be necessary for a Public Service Commission to be consulted (4) Nothing in clause (3) shall require a Public Service Commission to be consulted as respects the manner in which any provision referred to in clause(4) of article 16 may be made or as respects the manner in which effect may be given to the provisions of article 334.

❑

Appendix 2: Extracts of the USA Constitution

Pertaining to appointment and other duties of officers

Section 2

The President shall be Commander in Chief of the Army and Navy of the United States, and of the militia of the militia of the several States, when called into the actual service of the united States; he may require the opinion in writing, of the principal officer in each of the executive departments, upon any subject relating to the duties of their respective offices, and he shall have power to grant reprieves and pardons for offences against the United States, except in cases of impeachment.

He shall have power, by and with the advice and consent of the Senate, to make treaties, provided two thirds of the Senators present concur; and he shall nominate, and by and with the advice and consent of the Senate, shall appoint ambassadors, other public ministers and consuls, judges of the Supreme Court, and all other officers of the United States, whose appointments are not herein otherwise provided for, and which shall be established by law: but the Congress may by law vest the appointment of such inferior officers, as they think proper, in the President alone, in the courts of law, or in the heads of departments.

The President shall have power to fill up all vacancies that may happen during the recess of the Senate, by granting commissions which shall expire at the end of their next session

Section 4

The President, Vice President and all civil officers of the United States, shall be removed from office on impeachment for, and conviction of, treason, bribery, or other high crimes and misdemeanours.

❑

Appendix 3: Extracts of the Chinese Constitution

Relating to Public employment

No specific mention is made of public servants and services in the Chinese constitution. However, some connected references are given below:

Article 27

All state organs shall practice the principle of lean and efficient administration, a work responsible system, and a system of employee training and evaluation in order to keep improving the quality and efficiency of their work and combat bureaucratism.

All state organs and state employees must rely on the support of the people, stay engaged with them, listen to their opinions and suggestions, and accept their oversight and work hard to serve them

State employees when assuming office, should make a public pledge of allegiance to the Constitution in accordance with the provisions of law.

Article 44

The state shall in accordance with the provisions of law, implement a retirement system for employees of enterprises, public institutions and state organs. The livelihood of retirees shall be ensured by the state and society.

Article 48

Women in the People's Republic of China shall enjoy equal rights with men in all spheres of life: political, economic, cultural, social and familial.

The state shall protect the rights and interests of women, implement a system of equal pay for equal work, and train and select female officials.

Article 89

The State Council shall exercise the following functions and powers

17. to examine and decide on the size of administrative organs, and in accordance with law, to appoint, remove and train administrative officers, appraise their work and reward and punish them

Article 107

Local People's governments at and above the county level shall, according to the authority invested in them as prescribed by law, manage administrative work related to the economy, education, science, culture, public health, sport, urban and rural development, finance, civil affairs, public security, ethnic affairs, judicial administration, family planning etc, within their administrative areas; and shall issue decisions and orders, appoint or remove, train, evaluate, and award or punish administrative employees.

The people's government of townships, ethnic townships, and towns shall implement the resolutions of the people's congresses at their level and the decisions and orders of state administrative organs at the next level up; they shall manage the administrative work of their respective administrative areas. The people's governments of provinces and cities directly under central government jurisdiction shall decide on the establishment of townships and towns and their geographic division.

Article 109

Local people's governments at and above the county level shall establish audit offices. Local audit offices at all levels shall, in accordance with the provisions of law, independently exercise the power to conduct auditing oversight; they shall be responsible to the people's government at their level and to the audit office at the next level up.

Bibliography

1. Select Modern Government - V.D. Mahajan
2. Organizing China- The Problem of Bureaucracy – Harry Harding
3. Civil Service System in Asia – Edited by John P. Burns and Bidhya Bowornwathana
4. The Civil Service System of China: The Impact of the Environment- John P. Burns
5. The National Civil Service of India: A Critical View– R. K. Mishra

6. State of Connecticut- Register 1978

7. Dynamics of Bureaucracy- Peter M. Blau

Articles

1. Trysting with Destiny- Mohan Guruswamy (Economic Times-2020)

2. Covid-19 From the US, Lessons on what not to do- Frank F. Islam

❑❑❑